SCIENTISTS AND THEIR DISCOVERIES
LEONARDO DA VINCI

SCIENTISTS AND THEIR DISCOVERIES

ALBERT EINSTEIN

ALEXANDER FLEMING

ALFRED NOBEL

BENJAMIN FRANKLIN

CHARLES DARWIN

GALILEO

GREGOR MENDEL

ISAAC NEWTON

LEONARDO DA VINCI

LOUIS PASTEUR

THOMAS EDISON

SCIENTISTS AND THEIR DISCOVERIES
LEONARDO DA VINCI

JOHN CASHIN

MASON CREST

Mason Crest
450 Parkway Drive, Suite D
Broomall, Pennsylvania 19008
(866) MCP-BOOK (toll-free)
www.masoncrest.com

Copyright © 2019 by Mason Crest, an imprint of National Highlights, Inc.

All rights reserved. No part of this publication may be reproduced or transmitted in any form or by any means, electronic or mechanical, including photocopying, recording, taping, or any information storage and retrieval system, without permission from the publisher.

Printed and bound in the United States of America.

CPSIA Compliance Information: Batch #SG2018.
For further information, contact Mason Crest at 1-866-MCP-Book.

First printing
9 8 7 6 5 4 3 2 1

Library of Congress Cataloging-in-Publication Data

ISBN: 978-1-4222-4032-8 (hc)
ISBN: 978-1-4222-7764-5 (ebook)

Scientists and their Discoveries series ISBN: 978-1-4222-4023-6

Developed and Produced by National Highlights Inc.
Interior and cover design: Yolanda Van Cooten
Production: Michelle Luke

QR CODES AND LINKS TO THIRD-PARTY CONTENT
You may gain access to certain third-party content ("Third-Party Sites") by scanning and using the QR Codes that appear in this publication (the "QR Codes"). We do not operate or control in any respect any information, products, or services on such Third-Party Sites linked to by us via the QR Codes included in this publication, and we assume no responsibility for any materials you may access using the QR Codes. Your use of the QR Codes may be subject to terms, limitations, or restrictions set forth in the applicable terms of use or otherwise established by the owners of the Third-Party Sites. Our linking to such Third-Party Sites via the QR Codes does not imply an endorsement or sponsorship of such Third-Party Sites or the information, products, or services offered on or through the Third-Party Sites, nor does it imply an endorsement or sponsorship of this publication by the owners of such Third-Party Sites.

Publisher's Note: Websites listed in this book were active at the time of publication. The publisher is not responsible for websites that have changed their address or discontinued operation since the date of publication. The publisher reviews and updates the websites each time the book is reprinted.

CONTENTS

CHAPTER 1	Leonardo's Early Years in Florence	7
CHAPTER 2	The Emerging Scientist	21
CHAPTER 3	The Four Powers	33
CHAPTER 4	The Disciple of Experience	45
CHAPTER 5	Rome, City of Disillusion	63
CHAPTER 6	Final Years in France	75
	Chronology	84
	Further Reading	89
	Internet Resources	90
	Series Glossary of Key Terms	91
	Index	93
	About the Author	96

KEY ICONS TO LOOK FOR:

 Words to understand: These words with their easy-to-understand definitions will increase the reader's understanding of the text while building vocabulary skills.

 Sidebars: This boxed material within the main text allows readers to build knowledge, gain insights, explore possibilities, and broaden their perspectives by weaving together additional information to provide realistic and holistic perspectives.

 Educational videos: Readers can view videos by scanning our QR codes, providing them with additional educational content to supplement the text. Examples include news coverage, moments in history, speeches, iconic sports moments, and much more!

 Text-dependent questions: These questions send the reader back to the text for more careful attention to the evidence presented there.

 Research projects: Readers are pointed toward areas of further inquiry connected to each chapter. Suggestions are provided for projects that encourage deeper research and analysis.

 Series glossary of key terms: This back-of-the-book glossary contains terminology used throughout the series. Words found here increase the reader's ability to read and comprehend higher-level books and articles in this field.

A view of Florence, Italy, showing the cathedral dome. To the left there is a turreted tower bearing a smaller tower on top. This is the Palazzo Vecchio, or Old Palace, in which the governing council of Florence worked. Leonardo lived close to it for many years.

WORDS TO UNDERSTAND

anatomy—the science of the structure of the body.

Annunciation—the announcement by the angel Gabriel to the Virgin Mary that she would become the mother of Christ.

apothecary—a medieval druggist, predecessor of the modern pharmacist or chemist.

guild—a union of craftsmen that kept up standards of work and protected the interests of its members.

natural philosophy—the science of the physical properties of bodies, alive or non-alive.

physiology—the science of the life processes in animals and plants.

CHAPTER 1

Leonardo's Early Years in Florence

Leonardo da Vinci was born into rapidly changing times. During the first few decades of his life, European sailors were making contact with other cultures in Africa and Asia. The explosive power of gunpowder was being used in war. The appearance of the printed book made communication of ideas easier. Long-accepted views in religion, politics, art, and science were being challenged. This was a great period of "rebirth"—the Renaissance. Some of the new ideas of the Renaissance came from looking back to the writings of the great thinkers of ancient Greece. Leonardo, however, differed from the other great thinkers of his time in an important way—he looked to the future, as well as to the past.

During Leonardo da Vinci's lifetime, Italy was not a unified country as it is today. It consisted of five great city-states—Milan, Venice, Florence, Rome, and Naples, each ruled by powerful families. The rulers of these city-states—including the Medici family that controlled Florence—relied on hired soldiers called *condottieri* to maintain their power. But they also encouraged the arts, such as painting, sculpture, and architecture, to bring prestige to their kingdoms. Ancient manuscripts and printed books rapidly became precious possessions, and were collected into libraries. Each ruler surrounded himself with artists to paint pictures of him, architects to build monuments to glorify his achievements, and scholars to write about him in books.

Scan here to learn more about the city-states of Renaissance Italy:

At the time of Leonardo's birth, the ruler of Florence was Cosimo de' Medici. He was one of the richest men in Europe, having made his money from the wool trade and banking. Cosimo ruled Florence from 1434 until 1464. During these years there was a steady inflow of immigrants from Constantinople (now called Istanbul), due to fighting between Christians and Muslims there. These refugees spoke Greek and brought with them many precious Greek manuscripts. Cosimo established a school under a learned scholar named Marsilio Ficino, who was an authority on the Greek philosopher Plato. Cosimo's policies were carried on by his son Piero, who ruled from 1464 until 1469, and then by his grandson, Lorenzo, who ruled until 1492. Lorenzo de' Medici was such a successful ruler that he came to be called *Il Magnifico* ("the Magnificent").

Early Years

Leonardo was born on April 15, 1452, in the country village of Vinci. Vinci lies high up on Mount Albano, which stands in the valley of the River Arno, near the Italian city of Florence. Looking west from the village, he would have seen the Mediterranean Sea. Leonardo was illegitimate. His mother was a peasant girl named Caterina. His father, Ser Piero da Vinci, the son of a Florentine lawyer, was quickly persuaded to marry into a good family. His mother was married off

The fall of Constantinople in 1453 to the Turkish Ottoman Empire marked the end of the Eastern Roman Empire (or Byzantine Empire). A wave of Byzantine refugees fled to western Europe, bringing with them ancient writings of Greek and Roman civilization that had been lost in the West for centuries. This influx of knowledge about astronomy, architecture, art, and philosophy inspired and drove a growing interest in scientific discovery.

to a cowherd. Nothing more is known of her, though forty years later, Leonardo wrote about paying the funeral expenses of a woman called Caterina, who may have been his mother.

Leonardo's grandparents immediately took Leonardo into their care. Their son Francesco, who had never had a son himself, became so attached to Leonardo that he eventually left him a farm in his will.

After a few years, Ser Piero realized that his wife, Donna Albiera, would bear him no children. Meanwhile, the young Leonardo was growing into a beautiful and promising child and so Ser Piero took his natural son into his family.

A view of the villa in which Leonardo grew up, near the town of Vinci.

Leonardo's father spent much of his time in Florence. His house was within earshot of the roaring lions kept at the back of the Palazzo Vecchio, the city's government offices. Leonardo's interest in lions was lifelong. Years later, he related, "I once saw how a lamb was licked by a lion in our city of Florence, where there are always from twenty-five to thirty of them . . . With a few strokes of his tongue the lion stripped off the whole fleece with which the lamb was covered, and having thus made it bare, ate it."

Leonardo's education was unusual because he was not taught Latin or Greek. This made it difficult for him to mix with the learned people of Florence. He regretted this, and tried to teach himself. His early notebooks contain long lists of Latin words. But there are no lists of Greek words. He must have found this language too difficult. While Leonardo had many talents, the ability to learn languages was not among them.

Leonardo explained his own unusual outlook on the world by likening himself to one who arrives last at a fair. "I will do like one who, because of his poverty, is the last to arrive at the fair, and . . . takes all the things that others have already seen and not taken but refused as being of little value. I will load my modest pack with these despised and rejected wares, the leavings of many buyers." The "despised and rejected wares" Leonardo referred were the wonders of nature. We call this "science" today, but in Leonardo's time it was called **natural philosophy**. Few were interested in it, but to Leonardo it was something to marvel at.

Apprenticeship

During the fifteenth century, all craftsmen—whether painters, goldsmiths, sculptors, or architects—were strictly controlled by **guilds** that established their conditions of employment. In fact, painters were classed as manual workers and did not qualify for a guild of their own. They came under the Guild of Apothecaries and Doctors because it was from the **apothecaries** that they bought their paints. This guild also controlled the activities of physicians, surgeons, herbalists, distillers, undertakers, booksellers, and silk merchants. In 1466, when he was fourteen years old, Leonardo was sent to work for Andrea di Verrocchio, an artist with a workshop in Florence.

Leonardo's teacher, Andrea di Verrocchio.

Verrocchio was a man of all-around ability. Like Leonardo, he had no advantages of birth, wealth, or book learning. He was a skilled craftsman, a goldsmith, a sculptor, and a painter. By working with him, Leonardo improved at these skills and as an inventor of machines. Both Verrocchio and Leonardo were eager to explore the unknown.

Verrocchio was probably impressed by the story Ser Piero told of how he had asked Leonardo to make a painting on a shield, a round piece of wood that he wanted to give to a peasant on his estate. Leonardo took the piece of wood to his workroom where, Vasari related, he kept, "lizards, newts, maggots, snakes, butterflies, grasshoppers, bats, and other animals of that kind." Based on these, Leonardo "composed a horrible and terrible monster." When it was finished, Leonardo sent for his father. "When Ser Piero knocked at the door," wrote Vasari, "Leonardo opened it and told him to wait a little, and, returning to his room put the round panel in the light on his easel, and having arranged the window to make the light dim, he called his father in. Ser Piero taken unaware, started back, not thinking of the round piece of wood, or that the face which

A statue of the young Leonardo da Vinci in Florence. Contemporary accounts described Leonardo as being finely built, strong, and handsome.

he saw was painted, and was beating a retreat when Leonardo stopped him and said, 'This work has served its purpose; take it away as it has produced the effect intended.'" Ser Piero did take it away, and went and bought another piece of wood with a heart pierced by a dart painted on it. This he gave to a very satisfied peasant, while he sold Leonardo's painting for 100 ducats. This story shows us an important part of Leonardo's science of art—a close look at things in nature (like the lizards, newts and other animals he kept in his workroom) can provide the artist with the raw material for his paintings. These may be fantastic, like the monster that he painted, but they may also tell us a great deal more about nature itself.

Leonardo and Verrocchio began the search for this artistic representation of the "truth" by exploring two fields of human knowledge, human **anatomy** and perspective. Anatomy is the study of the structure of the body. Perspective is the study of how three-dimensional objects can be represented on a two-dimensional surface (e.g. a drawing on a sheet of paper), so that it shows how an onlooker would have seen the object from any given point.

A TALENTED PHYSICIAN

The republic of Florence under the Medici family produced many gifted citizens. The Florentines thought that a person should have a wide range of skills and interests. A person should be "whole and complete." People should not be limited in their outlook by their religion or profession.

Paolo Toscanelli, for example, was a physician but he spent much of his life studying astronomy and geography. In astronomy, he observed and plotted the course of the comets, including the one we now call Halley's Comet. His study of geography led him to send a letter to Columbus encouraging him to sail westward to China, "a country worth seeking by the Latins." This letter was written in 1478, when Leonardo lived in Florence.

Even though he was a physician, Toscanelli did not write about anatomy. The official teaching of anatomy to medical students was based on the works of Galen, an ancient Greek physician who had lived in the Roman Empire during the second century CE. In Leonardo's time, anatomy was still taught by demonstration only; students were not allowed to examine the bodies for themselves. But this barrier was eventually broken down by the artists of Florence. They wanted to portray the human body accurately, particularly the way the muscles were used. Examples of this can be seen in the works of Antonio Pollaiuolo. His studio was next door to that of Verrocchio, where Leonardo worked.

The study of perspective was not new. It had been first looked at by Filippo Brunelleschi, the architect who had finished the Florentine cathedral dome. The theory of perspective had been put into geometrical form by Leon Battista Alberti, who was still alive when Leonardo joined Verrocchio. The use of perspective was essential for anatomical drawings. For Verrocchio, the geometrical problems of perspective were too difficult, but they encouraged Leonardo to experiment for many years. Not until 1492, in Milan, was he able to set out the results of his experiments into rules of perspective, which he based on the physics of light.

In those days, it was the artists who studied anatomy, not doctors of medicine. Within a few yards of Verrocchio's workshop was an art studio managed by the Pollaiuolo brothers. They obtained their knowledge of human muscles mostly from flayed corpses—bodies from which the skin had been removed. Their example was followed by Verrocchio, who produced a statue of a flayed Greek god, Marsyas.

During his time with Verrocchio, Leonardo's interests broadened. Wandering in the countryside around Florence, his observant eye began to notice rock formations, caves, and fossils. What he saw in the layers of rock and their fossils raised questions in his mind. It was the same with plants. There in the valley of the Arno River, he began his botanical research. The results of these can be seen in his paintings of flowers and trees in his two earliest known paintings of the **Annunciation**. One is in the Louvre in Paris, the other in the Uffizi Gallery in Florence. Leonardo was enrolled in the Company of Painters in 1472.

Unhappy Years

In 1476, tragedy overtook Leonardo. For the whole of his life, he never seemed very interested in women except as mother figures. To many, this suggested that he was a homosexual. A charge was brought against him by an unknown person who placed an unsigned letter in the box in the wall of the Palazzo Vecchio provided for this sort of accusation. The charge was dismissed, but there is evidence in Leonardo's notebooks that it caused him great distress.

During this period, he painted a picture of Saint Jerome that is now in the Vatican. This shows the human mind and body at the limit of suffering. Not only does

Jerome beat his bruised chest with a stone, but his face is contorted with mental pain. Even the lion in the foreground roars in sympathy. It was at this time that Leonardo began to look at the nature and causes of pain. He wrote, "while the highest good is wisdom, the chief evil is bodily pain . . ." Later he noted that nature had placed the more sensitive parts of the body in front "for the preservation of man."

These observations and this painting remind us that human beings were the foundation of the science and the art of Leonardo. This led him very early to the study of human movements and proportions. Studies like these may have been even more interesting to him because of his own fine proportions. Vasari

Leonardo's unfinished painting St. Jerome in the Wilderness *shows the extreme suffering of the saint, partly through Leonardo's understanding of the anatomy of the face and neck muscles.*

described Leonardo's person and personality as follows: "The heavens often rain down the richest gifts on human beings naturally, but sometimes with lavish abundance bestow upon a single individual beauty, grace and ability. . . . Men saw this in Leonardo da Vinci whose personal beauty could not be exaggerated, whose every movement was grace itself, and whose abilities were so extraordinary that he could readily solve every difficulty. He possessed great physical strength combined with dexterity, and a spirit and courage invariably royal and magnanimous . . . The grace of God so possessed his mind, his memory and intellect formed such a mighty union, and he could so clearly express his ideas that he was able to confound the boldest opponents." And this from a man who admired Michelangelo much more than Leonardo!

Vasari ignored Leonardo's attitude to science. Leonardo was almost superhumanly capable of unbiased observation, not only of people and objects around him, but of himself. His notes are full of "discussions" between "opponents." Some of these are arguments he had with himself! In some of them, Leonardo repeated the opinions of others such as Aristotle. Sometimes he agreed with these views and sometimes he disagreed with them. But he never let his previous opinions cloud his judgment. Indeed, Leonardo was quite willing to base his own views and drawings on those made by others. But even when he did this, he often made improvements to their work!

Leonardo's intellectual powers may have set him apart from others and made him lonely, for he seems to have had few close friends. Yet, his kindness and sympathy were noticed by many. "He was very fond of horses," wrote Vasari, "and indeed he loved all animals and trained them with great kindness and patience. Often when passing places where birds were sold, he would let them out of their cages and pay the vendor the price asked." This love of animals made him a vegetarian. It also hindered his search for knowledge, for he hardly ever performed animal experiments. Had he done so, he might have made greater advances in **physiology**.

This was the Leonardo who left Verrocchio's studio in 1476, to make his own independent career.

His remaining years as a young man in Florence were not happy. His life had been scarred by the accusation made against him. Although he worked for a time for Lorenzo de' Medici as a sculptor, he did not mix with the aloof scholars of Florence. Nor did he want to. He did not agree with such artists as Marsilio Ficino or Pico della Mirandola, who publicly stated that "mathematics are not true knowledge."

Once more, Leonardo combined his studies of perspective with his studies of human beings. He made many drawings for a painting called the *Adoration*

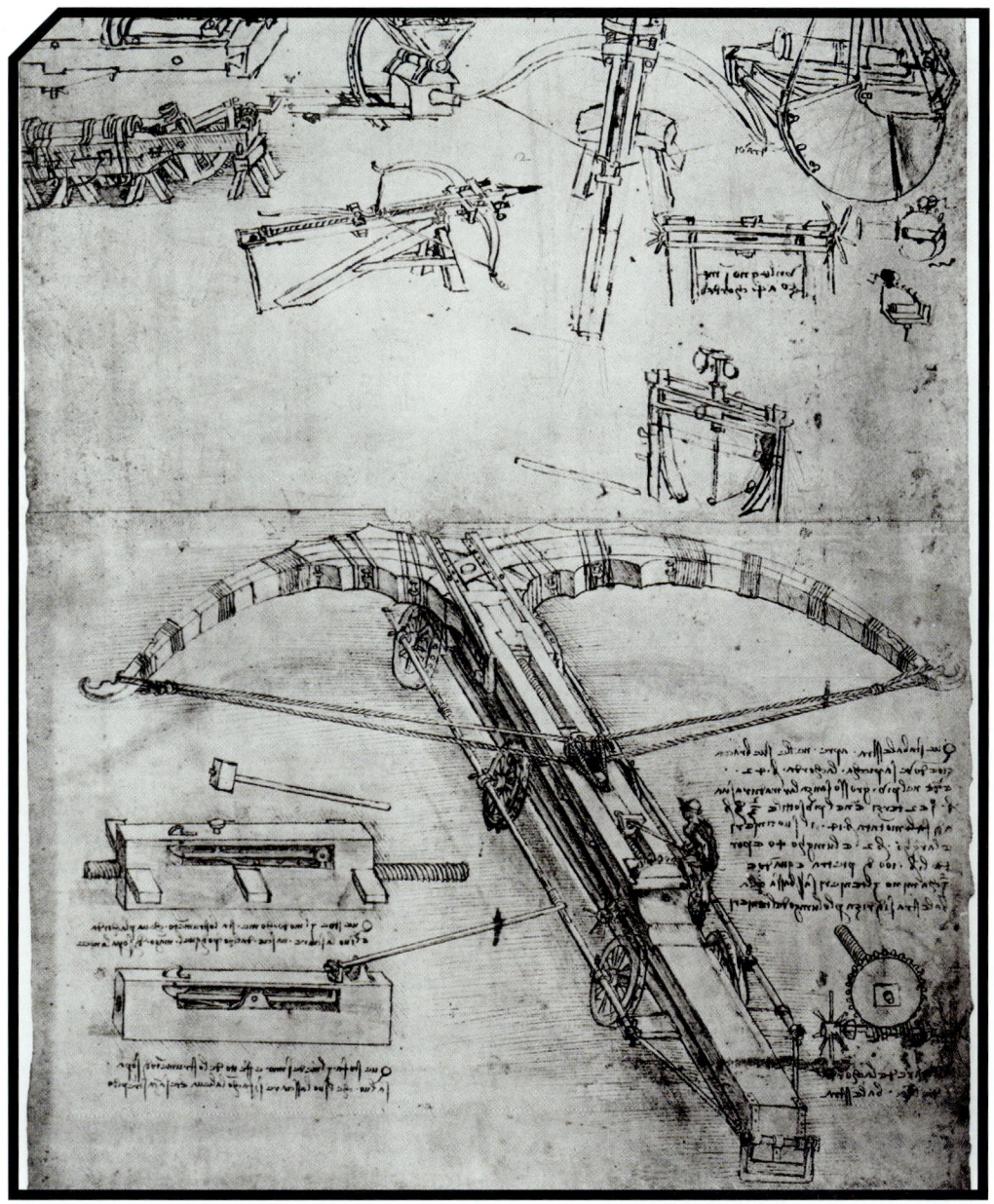

This page from one of Leonardo's notebooks shows a design for a giant crossbow. While renowned today as an artist, for much of his life Leonardo was interested in designing weapons and defensive fortifications. Throughout his lifetime, warfare was nearly constant on the Italian peninsula.

of the Magi that still hangs in the Uffizi Gallery in Florence. In it we can see his increasing mastery of his own ideal: "A good painter has two chief objects to paint, man and the State of his soul; the former is easy, the latter hard because he had to represent it by the attitudes and movements of the limbs."

During the years spent in Verrocchio's studio, Leonardo found many outlets for his mechanical genius. Florence at that time was a hub of creative arts. Problems involving building, sculpture, metal work, hydraulics, and problems involving war machines of all kinds were always being discussed. Leonardo was very good at inventing machines, and delighted in what we would call the technology of his day. It was part of his defense against the scholars of Florence to say that, "They go about puffed up and pompous, in fine raiment and bejeweled, not from the fruits of their own work but from those of others. My work they refuse to recognize. They despise me the inventor, but how much more are they to blame for not being inventors, but trumpeters and reciters of the works of others."

His claim to be an inventor was not an idle boast. It is proved by looking at some of his notes and drawings. An idea of how good an inventor he was is given in a letter he wrote to Ludovico Sforza, duke of Milan, in about 1481, offering his services. Here Leonardo wrote:

> I can construct bridges very light and strong, and capable of easy transportation, and with them you may pursue and on occasion flee from the enemy; and still others capable of resisting fire and attack, easy and convenient to place and remove; and methods of burning and destroying those of the enemy. . . .
>
> In times of peace I believe I can give perfect satisfaction, equal to that of any other in architecture and the construction of buildings both private and public, and in conducting water from one place to another. Also I can carry out sculpture in marble, bronze or clay; similarly in painting I can do whatever can be done as well as any other whoever he may be.

Leonardo was not bragging. Sketches and notes related to all of these things, as well as other projects that he proposed in the letter, can be found in Leonardo's notebooks. The duke of Milan was impressed, and invited Leonard to move to his city.

TEXT-DEPENDENT QUESTIONS

1. When was Leonardo born?

3. With what Florentine artist did Leonardo begin an apprenticeship in 1466?

6. What crime was Leonardo charged with in 1476?

RESEARCH PROJECT

Using your school library or the internet, research the life of Giorgio Vasari, a Florentine painter and architect who is most famous for his 1568 book *Lives of the Most Excellent Painters, Sculptors, and Architects*. Vasari's book included biographies of Leonardo and his teacher Andrea del Verrocchio. How would you characterize Vasari's attitude toward Leonardo, and artists from Florence in general? Write a two-page paper and share it with your class.

Sforza castle dominates the city of Milan. It was home to the ruling Sforza family, including Leonardo's patron, Duke Ludovico. Leonardo was hired to paint several frescoes to decorate the castle.

 **WORDS TO UNDERSTAND**

confraternity—a brotherhood that has a charitable or religious purpose.

convection current—a current that transfers heat from one place to another by mass motion of a fluid such as air, water, or molten rock.

macrocosm—the "great world," or universe.

optic nerve—the nerve from the eye to the brain through which the visual impressions pass.

CHAPTER 2

The Emerging Scientist

The Leonardo who went to Milan in 1482 was in the prime of life—a blond, blue-eyed athlete, thirty years old. "His personal strength was prodigious," wrote Vasari. "With his right hand he could bend the clapper of a knocker or a horseshoe as if they had been lead." His senses were also very keen, particularly his sight and hearing. Along with his strength, he combined great mechanical skill.

Already, Leonardo was accepted as a master painter, and highly thought of as an inventor. It was as an artist-engineer that Leonardo was to get jobs for the rest of his life. Even his official burial document in France refers to him as *"premier peintre et ingénieur et architecte du Roi"* ("first painter, engineer and architect to the King"). What was not recognized was that he made painting and engineering a science.

This change in Leonardo, from a technologist to a scientist, he brought about in himself during twenty years of hard struggle. Beginning as more of an artist than a scientist, Leonardo finished his life as more of a scientist than an artist. His manuscripts that have survived consist mostly of personal notes, that give a picture of his changing outlook.

Contract Painting

For some years after he went to Milan, Leonardo was frustrated. In Milan, as a Florentine, he was "a foreigner." The war with Venice, that Leonardo had in mind when he made his application to Duke Ludovico Sforza, had come to nothing. Leonardo, apparently, found no work as a painter until he

Leonardo's masterpiece The Virgin of the Rocks was painted between 1483 and 1486 to decorate the Chapel of the Immaculate Conception in Milan.

worked with a native of the city, Ambrogio de Predis. Together, they obtained a contract from a group of monks, the **Confraternity** of the Immaculate Conception, to paint a picture. The contract detailed exactly what the monks wanted in their painting.

What the monks received was a painting known as *The Virgin of the Rocks*, far richer in design, color, and feeling than anything they had imagined. Because of this, they did not want it. They accused Leonardo of not doing what they had asked and took him to court. The argument was not settled for over twenty years. This picture shows how Leonardo had progressed in his studies of light, shade, and perspective. Leonardo explained that the shapes of objects are not made up of lines but of differences in light and shade. Leonardo was able to paint these differences and produce the optical illusion of seeing real objects. What Leonardo did not explain was how he achieved the quality of the painting, which he called the "soul." This "spiritual" beauty is present in the faces and gestures of each figure in the picture.

Leonardo's painting ability was already far ahead of his time. But he was not so happy about his mastery of language. To remedy this he made himself a dictionary of words—some in Latin, some in Italian—and sometimes he grouped together words describing one subject. There are, for example, 400 words describing pain and suffering. It is at once noticeable that most of the 30,000 words listed in his notebooks are abstract, i.e. words that do not describe actual things but only ideas. It was in expressing his ideas that Leonardo had most difficulty. But it was this interest in words that led Leonardo to try and learn more about language, speech, and the voice itself. Twenty years after declaring that, "No voice can be produced without percussion, and there cannot be percussion without an instrument," he returned to the subject of the voice. He made detailed studies of the anatomy of the human larynx, tongue, and lips, and explained how these "instruments" make the sounds of words, and how that sound reaches the ear of the hearer.

Inventions

In his early years in Florence and Milan, Leonardo the technologist produced a mass of inventions. In one history of machinery published in 1899, 400 devices invented by Leonardo are described. It was during this period of his life that he

For a short explanation of painting techniques employed by Renaissance artists, scan here:

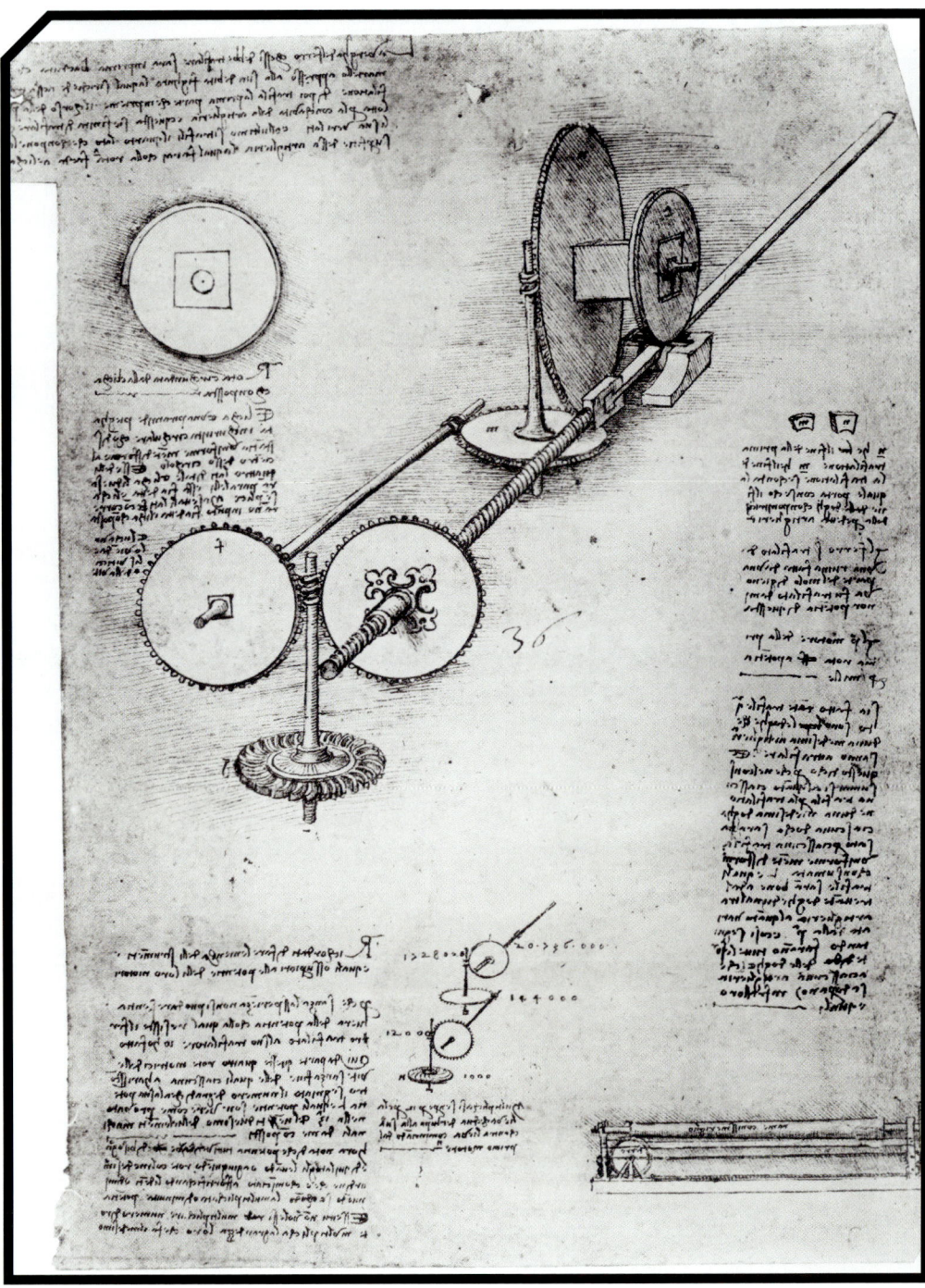

invented most, but he never stopped inventing until his death.

Some of Leonardo's earliest inventions were related to his studies of light and vision. A machine for lens grinding and polishing appeared as early as 1478–80. Methods of raising water using Archimedes's screw were devised at about this time also. One of his simplest and most ingenious inventions was his turn-spit for roasting meat. This was controlled by the **convection current** of warm air rising from the fire beneath. In the workshop itself, Leonardo gave a lot of thought to the tools that he used and was continually trying to increase his equipment. To this end, he invented file-making machines, treadle-operated lathes, mechanical saws, machines for boring horizontally or vertically and lifting devices. It is not by chance that Leonardo produced the first picture of modern industry—a cannon foundry.

Leonardo spent a lot of time gun-making and inventing flying machines. Guns interested Leonardo, not so much for their military uses, but because they enabled him to study projectiles moving at high speeds. He invented new breech-loading mechanisms, multiple-barreled guns, and a steam-powered gun that he called "Architronito." He also studied the action of gunpowder and made up his own formula.

Leonardo's work on flying machines came from a desire to imitate bird flight. All his early efforts used flapping wings. Later, he used the principle of the propeller, the helicopter, and finally that of the glider, but never the hot air balloon. Leonardo's attempts to achieve human flight show a gradual change from trial-and-error technology to science. It was only after his early failures that he came to realize that many factors were involved. After some years without success, he set about studying the bodies of birds. Systematically, he pinpointed their center

Opposite page: Leonardo wrote in his notebooks using a special kind of shorthand that he developed himself. Also, he often wrote backward, starting at the right side of the page and moving to the left. This may have been to keep from smudging the notes—Leonardo was left-handed—or it may have been a way he could prevent others from understanding his discoveries. This page shows a water-driven, gear-powered machine that could be used to manufacture cannon barrels.

of gravity and measured the span and area of their wings in relation to their body weight. He even calculated the amount of muscle a person would need to be able to flap "wings" and fly. When he realized the importance of a bird's tail for balancing and steering, he studied models of them and the effects air currents had on them. He then observed how a large bird often flies without beating its wings. "The wind which passes under the wing lifts it up just as a wedge lifts a weight. " He gave as an example, "the flight of cranes . . . which proceed to raise themselves by many turns after the manner of a screw . . . and a screw is of the nature of a wedge." But this observation came too late in his life for him to turn it into another practical invention. He never made a piloted glider.

Leonardo's study of water arose from his early attempts to use water power. Many of his drawings of waterwheels show them working machines such as mills and bellows for furnaces. Sometimes his drawings are based on the work

THE ARCHITECT AND THE HEALER

Leonardo saw the structure of buildings as similar to that of the human body. This is clearly shown in a letter he wrote to go with a model he submitted as a design for the dome of the Milan cathedral, in which he compared the work of an architect to that of a person who healed the sick. "You know that medicines when well-used restore health to the sick, and he that knows them well will use them well when he also knows what man is, what life and constitution are, and what health is," Leonardo wrote. "In just the same way a cathedral in need of repair requires a doctor-architect who understands well what a building is, on what rules the correct construction is based … and what the causes are that hold the structure together, what the nature of weight is and what the desire of strength is, and how these should be interwoven and bound together."

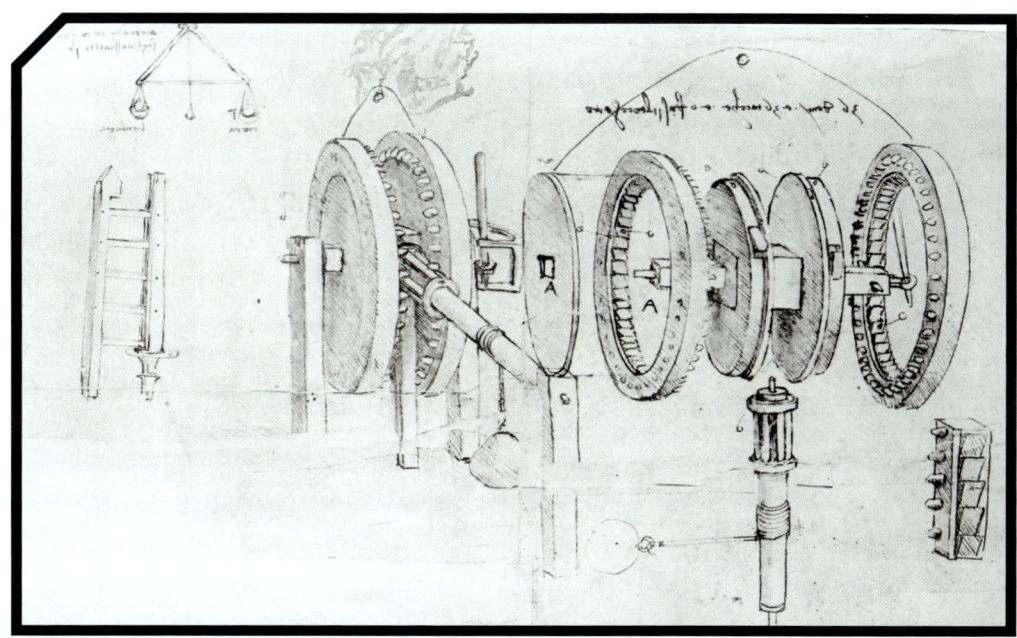

Reproduction of page from Leonardo's notebook showing a geared device for hoisting heavy loads safely; an "exploded view" on the right shows the relationship of the various parts. Leonardo was one of the first to use an "exploded view" to illustrate how his inventions should be built. Today, this is a common feature of most mechanical assembly manuals.

of others. The works of Vitruvius, the Roman architect and engineer, and of the Sienese engineers Francesco di Giorgio and Taccola, were known and admired by him. He took their ideas and often improved them. We have already mentioned how he used Archimedes's screw for raising water. He used Taccola's ideas for improving his own models of paddleboats. Leonardo also made detailed and ambitious plans for making canals with locks for transporting goods and for irrigation. He put these into practice in the canal system around Milan. He completed six new locks, including one at the end of the Martesana canal, creating a design that has been described as, "the first complete design of a modern lock—of highest importance in the history of canal construction."

In 1484, there was a terrible outbreak of Plague in Milan that forced Duke Ludovico and others to flee from the city in fear for their lives. Leonardo recognized that town planning would reduce the effect of these outbreaks. He proposed to the duke that ten small cities, each consisting of 5,000 houses and 30,000 people, should be built in the area around Milan. "In this way," he wrote, "you will distribute the masses of humanity who live crowded together like herds of goats filling the air with stench and spreading the seeds of plague and death." He made a number of drawings of such cities, with the towns planned on a network of canals that eventually drained into the nearest big river. Above the canals, which were used for trade, he designed roads with drains and public lavatories for pedestrians. However, Duke Ludovico ignored this ambitious plan for satellite towns around Milan.

Leonardo's notes of this period contain many architectural plans. Among his many designs for cathedrals are some closely related to Bramante's plan for the great cathedral of Saint Peter's in Rome. Bramante and Leonardo knew each other well in Milan. It is typical of Leonardo that his experiments in architectural problems began with a study of building tools and instruments. He also experimented on the strength of beams, pillars, and arches.

Medical and Artistic Studies

While in Milan, Leonardo briefly returned to his work on anatomy. This was partly due to his interest in the similarities he saw between buildings and the human body, but mainly it was because he wanted to continue his study of perspective. His experiments had shown him that there were marked differences in the size and shape of the "real object" and its image as seen by the eye. How did these come about? Was Plato right when he said that we cannot trust our senses? In the rules of perspective Leonardo found part of the answer, but he had to go on and study the structure of the eye and its relationship with the brain.

In 1489, he began a new notebook on human anatomy. It contains crude sketches of the eye, and of the **optic nerve** entering an equally crudely sketched brain. Apart from some splendid drawings of the orbit of the eye and skull, these early studies did little more than open the doors of a vast new world for Leonardo. But he was not ready to explore this new world yet, not until he had made more progress in discovering the "rules" of physics that governed

Tourists view Leonardo's The Last Supper *in the refectory of the Convent of Santa Maria delle Grazie in Milan. This masterpiece required about three years to paint.*

the outside world (or **macrocosm**). For nearly twenty years, he abandoned his human anatomical research. Then he returned to it, armed with his newly discovered "rules" of the "four powers" of nature.

In the meantime, he concentrated on the anatomy of the horse. In his application to Ludovico Sforza, Leonardo had offered to make a bronze horse to the "immortal glory" of Ludovico's father, Duke Francesco. As usual, Leonardo's preparations were so thorough that Duke Ludovico thought that he would never finish the job and toyed with the idea of getting someone else to do it. Leonardo was busy working out the most imposing attitudes of a huge bronze horse about twenty-six feet high. He was also dissecting horses so that he would be able to show the power of his fine horse better than had ever been done before.

In the end, Leonardo did produce a huge clay model of a horse. Ludovico put it in the courtyard of his castle to celebrate the marriage of his niece, Bianca Maria Sforza, to the future Emperor Maximilian I. The colossal horse took people's breath away. Its size and its snorting nostrils seemed to shout "force" (Sforza) to all who saw it. For six years, it stood in the castle courtyard. Leonardo was still trying to work out how to cast it in bronze when the French Army, intent on conquering Milan, arrived at the city in 1498. The French archers thought the great horse an excellent target for archery practice, and shot it to pieces.

Before the French invasion, Leonardo again turned his science into art. Around the year 1495 he painted a mural titled *The Last Supper* on the wall of the dining hall of the monastery attached to Santa Maria della Grazie—Duke Ludovico's favorite church.

Once more, Leonardo worked passionately, but slowly, to put all his knowledge of perspective and the human body into the work. Sometimes he would paint for a whole day without eating, at other times he would stand looking at his picture for hours, and leave without touching it with his brush. He chose to paint the moment when Jesus Christ said to his disciples, "One of you will betray me," as described in the Biblical Gospel of John. Leonardo showed the wave of shock passing over the faces of the apostles, who were seated on either side of Jesus. All of them take the emotional shock in a different way according to their character. One of the apostles, Judas, is all in the shadow, his face and hands twisted with grief and shame.

By 1499, Duke Ludovico had been defeated by the French and driven into exile. With the city in turmoil, Leonardo also left Milan, accompanied by his friend Luca Pacioli. Pacioli was a mathematician who had taught Leonardo about Euclid's geometry and arithmetic—how to find square roots, for example. It was through his friendship with Pacioli that Leonardo came to value mathematics—and particularly geometry—so highly. Leonardo came to see geometry behind all of nature. He wrote, "Let no man who is not a mathematician read the elements of my works," and "There is no certainty where one cannot apply any of the mathematical sciences." He also wrote that, "Mechanics are the Paradise of the mathematical sciences because here one comes to the fruits of mathematics."

TEXT-DEPENDENT QUESTIONS

1. When did Leonardo arrive in Milan?
3. What were some of Leonardo's inventions?
5. What is the Archimedes's screw?
7. What unfinished project did Leonardo work on for Duke Ludovico Sforza in Milan?

RESEARCH PROJECT

Using your school library or the internet, find out more about the life of Roman architect and engineer Vitruvius. Write a two-page report about his accomplishments and the things Leonardo learned from them, and present it to your class.

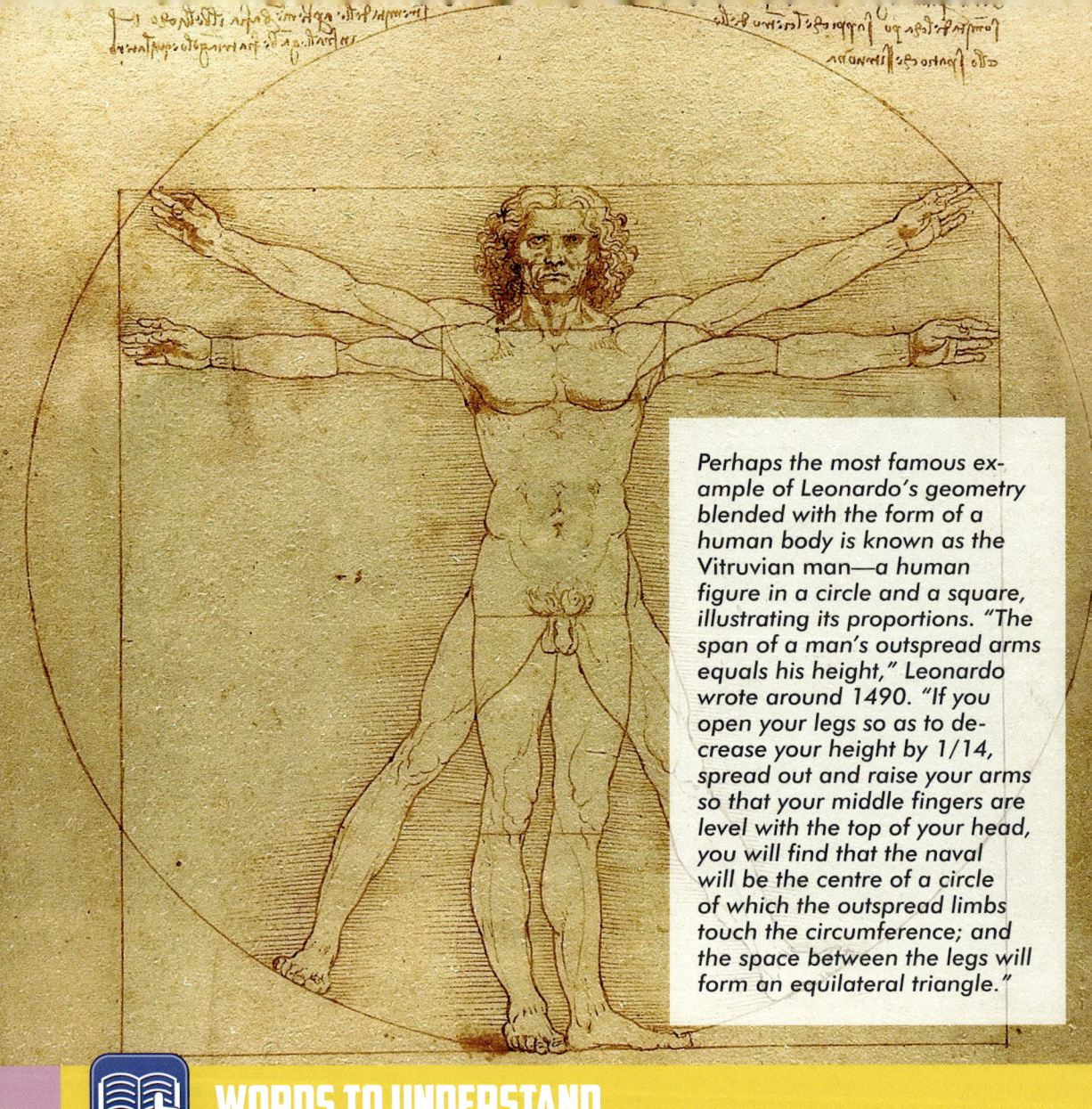

Perhaps the most famous example of Leonardo's geometry blended with the form of a human body is known as the Vitruvian man—a human figure in a circle and a square, illustrating its proportions. "The span of a man's outspread arms equals his height," Leonardo wrote around 1490. "If you open your legs so as to decrease your height by 1/14, spread out and raise your arms so that your middle fingers are level with the top of your head, you will find that the naval will be the centre of a circle of which the outspread limbs touch the circumference; and the space between the legs will form an equilateral triangle."

WORDS TO UNDERSTAND

accidental movement—movement produced by forces other than natural forces.

impetus—defined by Leonardo as, "a power impressed by the mover on a moved object."

natural movement—movement produced by natural forces such as gravity (weight) or "levity" (lightness).

CHAPTER 3

The Four Powers

In around 1490, Leonardo's notes changed from being mainly descriptions of inventions, to being a record of his search for the principles underlying how those inventions would work. He began to look for what he called "rules." He discussed at length ways of obtaining knowledge, and considered arguments about the value of observation, experimentation, and the relation of cause and effect. Leonardo's writings indicate that he was gradually changing from an artist-inventor into a scientist. His interest included the mechanism of the entire "terrestrial machine," as he called the earth.

Leonardo defined science as knowledge of things present, past, and possible. He readily turned to the past for a better understanding of the nature of things—to Aristotle, Archimedes, and Euclid in particular. All of them were ancient Greek philosophers and mathematicians.

In Leonardo's time, the study of theology, or religious doctrine, was said to be the "queen of the sciences." Knowledge that was gained through experience was said to be full of error and mostly worthless. Leonardo disagreed. While he called God the "prime mover," he believed that God acted through nature in a logical way. Further, he wrote, "all our knowledge has its origins in our senses." For Leonardo the artist, vision was the most important of the senses. "The painter," he wrote, "contends with and rivals Nature," and "The eye, the window of the soul, is the chief means whereby the understanding can most fully and abundantly appreciate the infinite works of Nature; and the ear is second."

But at the same time, Leonardo was well aware that the human eye can be tricked. He had already carried out many experiments on perspective. With

A bust of Archimedes in a park in Rome. The Greek mathematician and engineer Archimedes (c. 287–212 BCE) is remembered for his discovery of the "Archimedes principle" of bodies in water, and for his machines of war.

these he sorted out the causes of false appearances (optical illusions) from "true" ones. These experiments had made clear to him the conditions in which the true proportions of things can be seen—and then reproduced by the painter. This "natural" perspective, he claimed, allows "the mind of the painter to transform itself into the very mind of Nature, to become an interpreter between Nature and Art. It explains the causes of Nature's manifestations as compelled by its laws."

Light travels in straight lines. So does vision. From his observations of light and shadows, Leonardo concluded that perspective operated on light in the same way as on a person's vision. He believed that if light obeys the law of perspective, then, "perspective must be preferred to all the discourses and systems of human learning." Leonardo would not make such an astonishing statement without good cause. He felt that through his own work on perspective, he had discovered and proved a basic law of light. Its power is reduced in the form of a pyramid as it travels in circles outward from a luminous object.

During the 1490s, Leonardo was also making experiments on the movement of water. He observed that, "If you throw a stone into the water it becomes the center and cause of many circles . . ." and "If you throw two small stones at the same time on to a sheet of motionless water at some distance from one another you will see that around the two percussions two quantities of separate circles are caused, which as they increase in size will meet and then penetrate and intersect one another, whilst all the time maintaining as their respective centers the places percussed by the stones." Leonardo used the word "percussion" to mean a blow or impulse.

These two experiments encouraged Leonardo to make a thorough investigation of how waves move through water. He concluded that, "the quick opening and closing of the water produced by the percussion of the stones is better described as a tremor than a movement." He showed this by placing blades of straw on the water. When ripples were made on the water, it could be seen that the blades of straw did not move from their original position. This was because the ripples were not made by the movement of the water itself, but by the movement of the tremor from one part of the water to another. Leonardo found that as the tremor passed through the water, its power gradually lessened.

Leonardo said that these wave movements were the same as those that took place in air—with light and with sound. "Although voices penetrating the air

The mathematician Euclid lived in Alexandria, Egypt, during the fourth century BCE, when Greeks ruled that region. His book Elements *is the oldest existing mathematical textbook; it influenced many European scientists, from Leonardo to Galileo and Isaac Newton.*

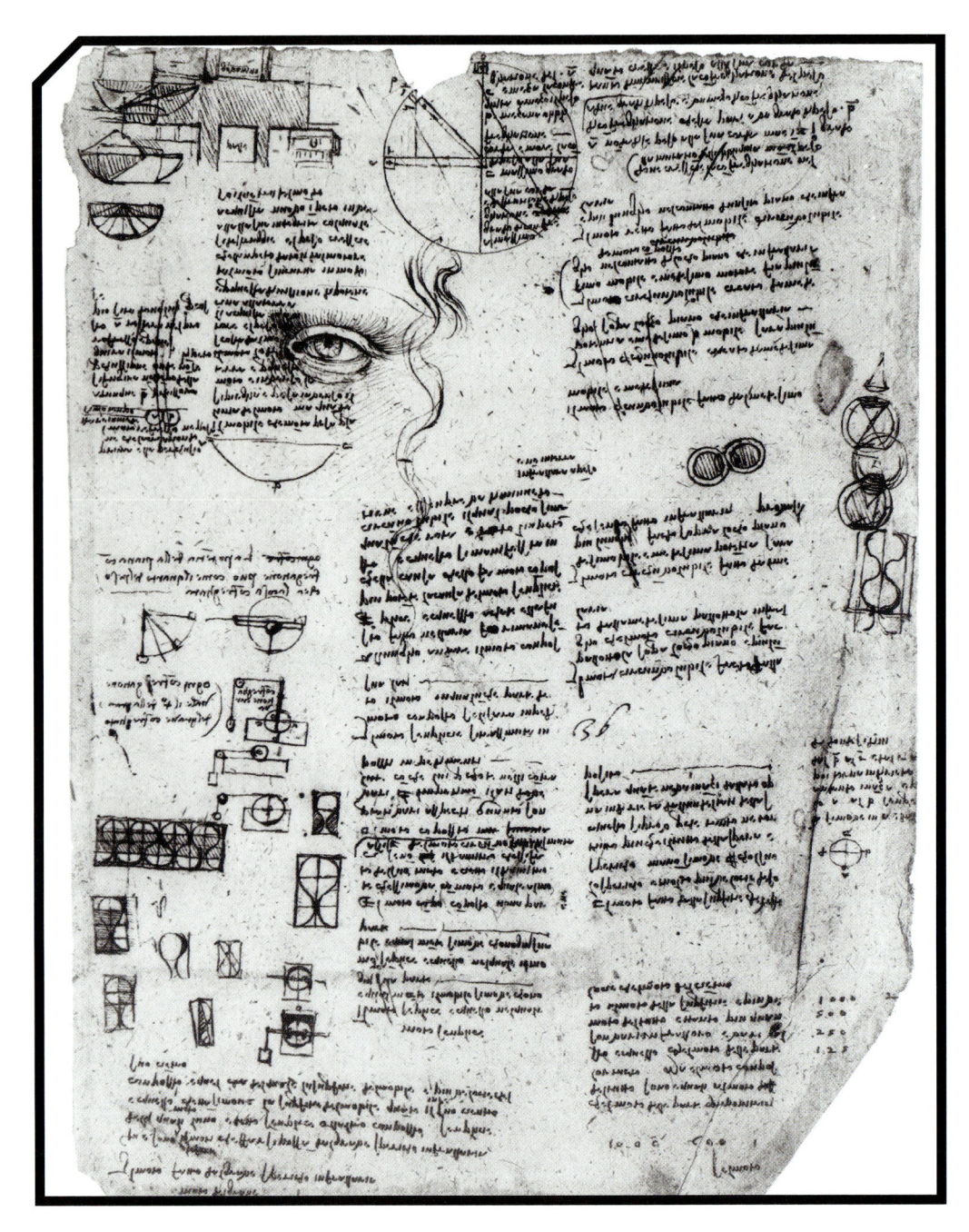

This page from Leonardo's notebooks includes some of his observations on the eye and vision.

spread in circular movement from their causes, none the less the circles moved from different centers meet and penetrate and pass into one another without impediment, always keeping to their causal centers. Because in all instances of movement there is great similarity between water and air."

How do these "pyramidal" and "circular" movements combine? Leonardo answered this question with a diagram, noting, "Every body in light and shade fills the surrounding air with infinite images of itself. These by infinite pyramids diffused in the air represent this body throughout space, in every part. Each pyramid that is composed of a long convergence of rays includes within itself an infinite number of pyramids . . . The circle [is] made by equidistant converging pyramidal rays making equal angles. And the eye will receive there objects of equal size."

This presented an entirely original wave theory of light. He used this wave pattern of forces in space to explain all other forms of power or energy known to him—sound, heat, and even the power of a magnet. All these wave forces for Leonardo lessened "pyramidally" from their source as they spread outward in circles.

We can now see why Leonardo was so interested in Euclid's geometry. He saw the whole of the Earth as made up of geometrical patterns. The "four elements," the skies above, the mountains and seas below, he saw as made up of geometrical shapes, just as a man-made cathedral is built up from the geometrically shaped stone blocks, bricks and beams. The forces of weight and pressure on these beams and blocks he saw in terms of the laws of the lever. The dynamic forces of movements in the "terrestrial machine" he saw, too, as geometrical patterns. And this, whether the body was alive or dead. He was sure that the same laws underlie the movements of a stone, or a living person.

Just as Leonardo accepted the four elements—earth, air, fire and water—he also accepted the Aristotelian physical forces of movement. Aristotle had held that, except for **natural movements** (caused by the "powers" of weight), all movements needed a mover or force. These were **accidental movements**. Leonardo broke new ground in adding to these "percussion," the word he used for a blow or impulse. This he called, "the immense power generated in the elements." He considered percussion to be more important and greater than any of the other powers generated in the four elements of nature; because, "Percussion in equal time exceeds any other power." It concentrates greatest force into least time. His many experiments into the relationship of percussion to the other forces, and its part in the movements of the four elements led him to rules such as, "Percussion is greatest along its central line." This rule can be shown to be true by thinking of a tennis ball hitting a wall. The ball will hit the wall more powerfully when thrown straight at it ("along its central line") than if it is thrown at an angle. Another rule, "The angle of incidence of percussion always equals the angle of reflection," he applied not only to light and cannon balls, but to the movements of water in rivers, and of blood in the heart—even to a man leaping on to his toes or heels.

A further force that was not in Aristotle's world of physics is one called **impetus**. Leonardo almost certainly got this idea from works written in the fourteenth century. He defined it as, "a power impressed by the mover on the moved

LEONARDO'S LIBRARY

Considering that Leonardo did not have a formal education in Greek and Latin, it may seem surprising to learn that this "uneducated" man possessed a large library of 116 books. Leonardo taught himself Latin grammar and increased his Italian vocabulary in order to read these books. He explained his reasons for these efforts by writing, "the natural desire of all good men is to know." He also wrote, "I know that many will call this [working so that he could understand these ancient texts] useless work . . . men who desire nothing but material riches and are absolutely devoid of that wisdom, the food and only true riches of the soul . . . And often when I see one of these men take this work in hand I wonder that he does not put it to his nose like a monkey, or ask me if it is good to eat."

Scan hear to learn more about one of Leonardo's most famous drawings:

thing." At the same time, he made many studies of friction. Friction causes a moving object to lose power and Leonardo stated that for smooth surfaces, the coefficient of friction (that is, the proportion of the power that is lost) is ¼. This is approximately right. Because he believed that there was no movement in nature that did not meet with resistance or friction, Leonardo's concept did not quite match Newton's later idea of inertia. Newton's theory was that every body continues in a state of rest or uniform motion in a straight line unless outside forces change that state. For Leonardo, however, all "impetus" gradually came to an end "pyramidally." He did, however, state repeatedly that in all the elements "action equals reaction," and, "The movement of air against a fixed thing equals the movement of a moved thing against immovable air. And it is the same in water." For example, "Movement of water against an oar equals the movement of the oar against water." Here he anticipated Newton's third law. In this, Newton stated that to every action there is an equal and opposite reaction. Leonardo's work on friction led him to use his new knowledge on his machines by introducing oiling points. He was also the first to use ball bearings to reduce friction.

Leonardo had a genius for devising experiments. He was also very patient and could keep repeating experiments with only small variations each time without becoming bored. These were designed to give him "rules" for the limited sets of conditions that he used in his experiments. Looking back on his own early inventions, he wrote, "Those who practice without science are like sailors who go to sea in a ship without rudder or compass. Practice must always be built on sound theory." On the other hand, he realized that, "The supreme misfortune is when theory outstrips practice."

Leonardo's experiments were meant to measure the relationship between cause and effect. To do this Leonardo needed measuring instruments. Thus, we find his notebooks full of designs for clocks of many varieties, of flow meters, compasses, anemometers for measuring wind speed, hygrometers for measuring humidity, etc. Many were copies or modifications of well-known instruments. An example of this was the hodometer for measuring mileage that he borrowed from Vitruvius. By applying his rules of perspective to his measurements of mileage, Leonardo was able to draw maps to scale.

Measurements in Leonardo's day were not standardized. There could be a considerable difference from one Italian city to the next in the weight of a pound or the length of a *braccio* (a measurement of length used in the Italian states at this time). Leonardo made a note, for example, that, "a pound in the Valtellina valley equals thirty ounces." A braccio could vary in length from fifteen to thirty-nine inches, so in his writings Leonardo carefully defined his use of this measurement as "the distance between the shoulder and the wrist." This was about twenty-four inches (0.6 meters).

Given this problem, how did Leonardo make any worthwhile measurements at all? He used proportions. For example, in his measurements of height in

Opposite page: A page from a mathematics book by Luca Pacioli (1447–1517), Summa de arithmetica. *The two men had a strong friendship, working and living together in several different cities for over a decade. Leonardo provided illustrations used in* Summa de arithmetica, *a groundbreaking work that included information about algebra, bookkeeping, and basic geometry.*

Ad illustrissimum Principem Gui. Vbaldum Vrbini Ducẽ Montis feretri: ac Durantis Comitem. Grecis latinisq; litteris Ornatissimum: & Mathematice discipline cultorum feruentissimum: Fratris Luce de Burgo sancti Sepulchri: Ordinis minorũ: & sacre Theologie Magistri. In arte arithmetice: & Geometrie. Prefatio.

A quantita Magnanimo Duca: e si nobile & excellẽte cosa che molti phylosophi per questo lbano giudicata ala substantia para: ecõessa coeterna. Peroche bano cognosciuto per verũ modo alcuna cosa in verũ natura senga lei nõ potere existere. per la qual cosa de lei irẽdo (cõ laiuto de colui che li nostri sensi reggi) tractarne: nonche per altri prischi e antichi phylosophi nonne sia copiosamente tractato: e in theorica e pratica. Ma per che lor dicti gia ali tempi nostri sonno molto obscuri: e vamolti male apresi: e ale pratiche vulgari male applicati: diche i lor operationi molto variano: e con grandi elaboriosi affanni mettano in opera: si de numeri cõmo de misure: vnde di lei parlando non intendo se non quãto che ala pratica e operare sia mestiero: mescolandoci secõdo iluoghi oportuni ancora la theorica: e causa de tale operare: si de numeri cõmo de geometria. Ma prima accio meglio qllo che sequita se habia apprẽdere: essa quantita diuid iremo secõdo el nostro proposito: e diuidendola a ciascun suo membro assegnaremo sua propria e vera diffinitione e descriptione. E aloza poi sequira quello che Arist. dici in secundo poster. Tsic enim maxime scimur aliquid cum habetur suum quid est &c.

Diffinitiones & diuisio discrete & continue quantitatis: articulus primus prime distinctionis.

Dico adõca. La quãtita essere imediate bimembre: cioe continua e discreta. La continua e quella lechui parti sonno copulate e gionte a certo termine cõmune: cõme sono legni: ferro: e sara &c. La discreta oueramẽte numero: e qlla lecui parti nõ sono giõte adalcuno termine cõ: cõmo e. 1. 2. 3. &c. Diche prima dela discreta: cioe del numero: e poi dela continua cioe geometria: quã to alo intento aspecta chiaramente tractaremo.

Diffinitio numeri proprianima: articulus secundus.

Numero: e (secondo ciascuno phylosophãte) vna multitudine de vnita cõposta: et essa vnita nõ e numero: ma ben principio de ciascun numero: ede qlla mediãte laqle ogni cosa e dicta essere vna. E secõdo elseuerin Boetio ĩ sua musica: e la vnita ciascũ nũero i potẽtia: & passiq i la sua arithmetica Regina e fondamento dogni numero lapella. Laqual piu magnificandola in le cose naturali disse in quello che sa de vnitate & vno. Omne quod est: ideo est: quia vnum numero est. Ene ancora el numero in infiniti menbri diuiso: per quel che esso Aristo. dice: cioe. Siquid infinitum est: numerus est. E per la terça petitione del septimo de Euclide: la su a serie in infinito potere procedere: et quocũq; numero vato: dari pót maior: vnitarem addendo. Ma noi pigliaremo quelle parti a noi piu note e accomodate. E pero dico con gliualtri alcuno essere primo: ede quello che solo vala vnita e numerato: e non ha altro numero: che integralmente aponto lo para. Altro e ditto cõposto: ede quello che da altro numero e mesurato: ouero numerato. Exẽplum primi cõmo. 3. 7. 11. 13. e 17. &c. Exemplu secũdi. cõmo. 4. chel voi lo mesura e numera: e. 8. chel. 2. e. 4. El. 12. 14. 18. e simili: tutti sono ditti numeri composti: nõ solo che constitu

a

relation to distance in studying perspective, the results are almost always given as proportions. He measured the distance from the viewer at which an object seemed to lose ½ of its height or ¾ of its height. These distances could be checked.

Leonardo preferred to experiment using models. This came naturally to an inventor of machines. For example, he made glass vessels of all shapes to observe the movements of water under different conditions. Markers of all kinds were used to show these movements more clearly. Grains of grass seed were popular, but he often used inks or small pieces of paper, too. He used dust and even leaves to detect the movements of air or water. He devised markers weighted to float at different depths in water to measure the speeds of currents of water at different levels. He dropped in weights on movable sticks to see the shape and speed of eddies. By using markers, he showed the destructive effects of rivers on their banks and the direction of the currents of blood flowing from the heart into the great artery of the body, the aorta.

Through his observations and experiments, and his geometrical theories of the workings of the "powers" of nature, Leonardo believed he could reach nature's innermost secrets. He tested his theories by using them. He made models and machines. He built canals and locks, and above all made pictures of reality through painting. His many successes encouraged him; his failures stimulated him to more research.

TEXT-DEPENDENT QUESTIONS

1. What was said to be the "queen of the sciences" in Leonardo's time?
5. Why was Leonardo so interested in Euclid's geometry?
6. How did Leonardo use his understanding of friction in his inventions?
7. What were Leonardo's rules of perspective?

RESEARCH PROJECT

Using the internet or your school library, find out about the accomplishments of Aristotle, an ancient Greek scholar whose ideas about physical science formed the basis for education in the Medieval and Renaissance periods of European history. Write a two-page report and share it with your class.

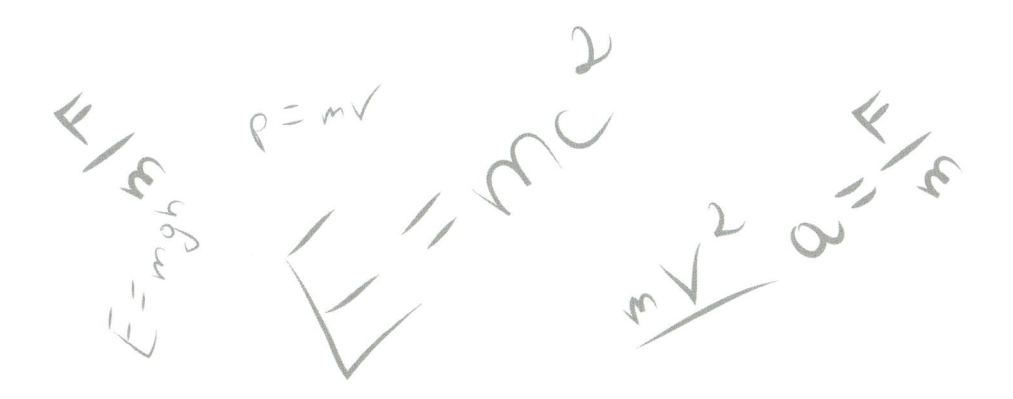

Statue of Leonardo da Vinci in the Piazza della Scala, Milan.

WORDS TO UNDERSTAND

cartoon—a preparatory drawing or sketch on strong paper for copying later as a fresco or painting.

cornea—the transparent membrane that forms the front covering of the eye.

heliocentric—an astronomical model of the solar system in which the sun is at the center and is orbited by the planets, including Earth.

microcosm—the "small world" of the human body.

CHAPTER 4
The Disciple of Experience

After his long stay of eighteen years in Milan, Leonardo became a wanderer. First, he went to Venice. The Ottoman Turks, who had defeated the Venetian fleet at Lepanto in 1499, were threatening to advance toward Venice over land. The alarmed Venetians asked Leonardo for his advice on strengthening their defenses. Leonardo gave them a plan to flood the Isonzo River on their frontier. He also designed a diving suit, which would allow the Venetians to bore holes in Turkish ships and sink them. Then, in 1500, he left for Florence.

Back in his native city, he was immediately asked to paint an altarpiece for the monastery of the Servite brotherhood. Their affairs at this time were being managed by Leonardo's father, Ser Piero. But Leonardo did not want to paint. Although he lodged in the monastery with the monks, instead of painting he studied geometry with his friend Luca Pacioli and helped him with the pictures for a book.

Eventually, the monks did persuade him to make a **cartoon** (a preliminary drawing) of the proposed artwork, called *The Virgin and Child with St. Anne and St. John the Baptist*. "This not only filled every artist with wonder," wrote the art biographer Vasari, "but when it was finished and set up in the room, men and women, young and old flocked to see it for two days as if it had been a festival, and they marveled exceedingly."

Is it just by chance that this picture was designed in the form of a pyramid? And that the balance of the Virgin sitting on Saint Anne's knee is in agreement

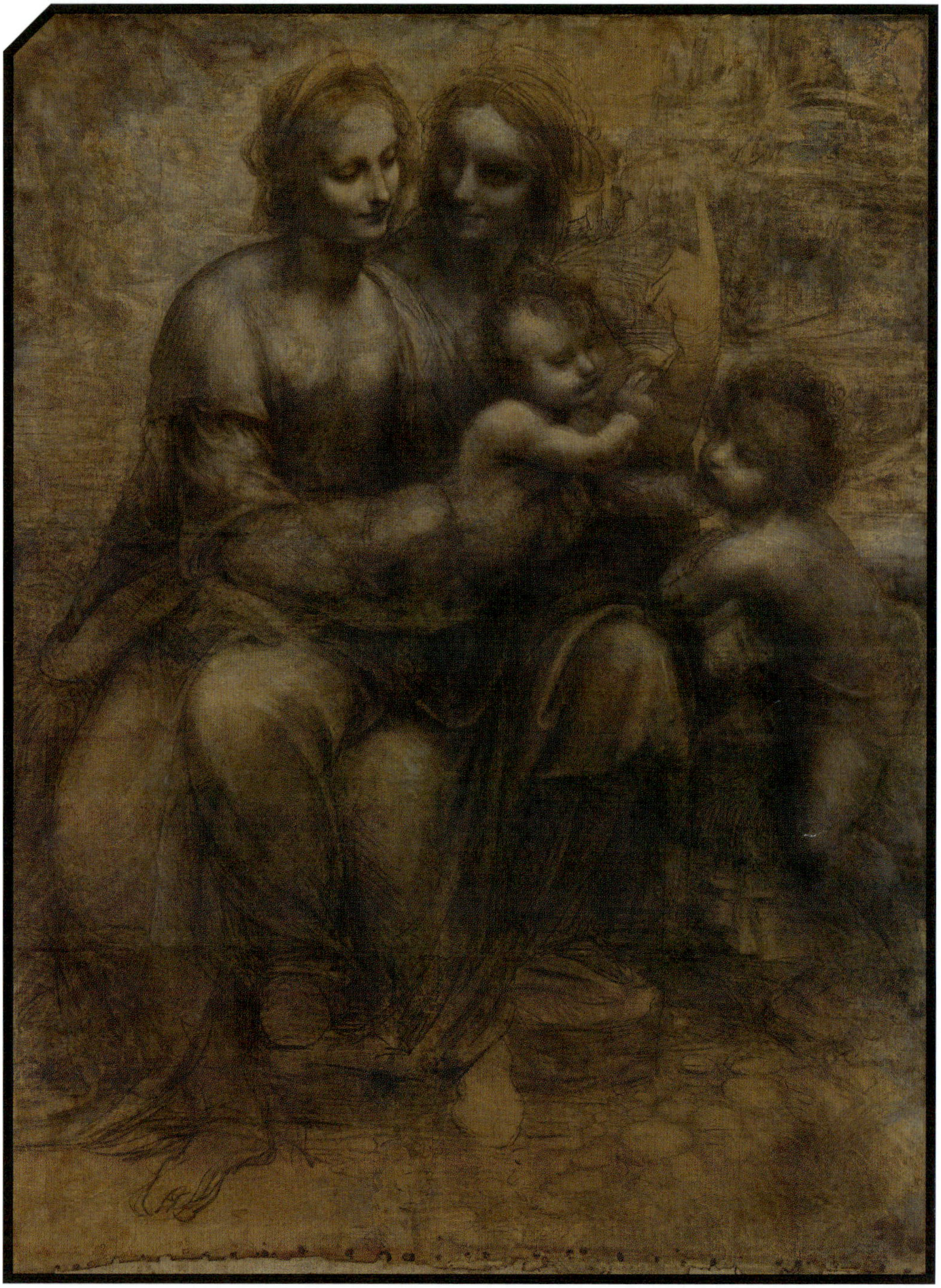

with the principles of the lever? Soon after, one of his admirers wrote, "Leonardo has lost all patience with the brush, and is now working entirely at geometry."

What did tempt Leonardo to stop working on geometry was a 1502 message from Cesare Borgia, asking him to serve as an engineer to his army. Borgia, the illegitimate son of Roman Catholic Pope Alexander VI, had been placed in charge of the Church's army and given lands to rule in central Italy, if he could conquer them. Leonardo had been studying the theory of military science for a long time and he was now keen to put it into practice. "First study science, then the practice arising from that science," he wrote. Cesare Borgia was giving him a chance to put his new theories into practice, and he accepted.

Portrait of Caesar Borgia (1475–1507), an infamous Italian condottiero *who ruthlessly sought power.*

The notebook that Leonardo kept during the next eight months contains no direct reference to Cesare Borgia's campaign. There are notes on the flight of birds, the drainage of marshes, bridge building, the building of forts, the formation of waves, and ideas for making maps. During his travels across Italy with Borgia, he drew the first scale maps, that would be useful in planning military campaigns. This led him to study the formation of the earth.

The unexpected death of Pope Alexander VI in August 1503 dealt a severe blow to Cesare Borgia's hopes of establishing his own kingdom in central Italy. The

Opposite page: Leonardo's cartoon for The Virgin and Child with St Anne and St John the Baptist, *created around 1501 in Florence. While the biographer Vasari says that many people admired this cartoon, Leonardo never completed the actual painting.*

next pope, Julius II, withdrew the Church's support and ordered him to withdraw from the territories he had invaded.

Return to Florence

Leonardo returned to Florence in 1503. A Florentine diplomat named Niccolò Machiavelli, whom Leonardo had met while working for Borgia, persuaded the government of Florence to send Leonardo to visit the camp of a Florentine army that was besieging the nearby city-state of Pisa. Leonardo's studies of water were now put to the test. He was asked to divert the Arno River so that Pisa would lose its water supply. Leonardo made detailed maps of the district and created a plan. To the alarm of the Pisans, a canal was dug that took the water of the Arno toward Leghorn. But when the canal was nearly finished, the floodwaters burst over the banks into its old course and Pisa was saved.

During these years, Leonardo had been carrying out many experiments on water. As always, he wanted to combine practice with theory. One notebook was intended to contain his whole science of water. Leonardo described it as, "On the nature of water in itself and its movements." Although he planned many sections of his book, none of them were completed. This was typical of Leonardo. What began as an ordered study soon became a huge mass of observations and experiments. Among these were analyses of waves and eddies, the formation of the world, the nature of fossils, the circulation of water in the earth, the formation of water vapor and the production of steam power.

Leonardo's studies of the scattering of sunlight by waves led him to think that the light of the moon was produced in a similar way. Noting that reflections from waves are scattered in all directions, Leonardo suggested that there must be water waves on the moon. And, if there were waves, there must be wind to cause them. From this argument, he concluded that the moon was like the Earth in having its own atmosphere held by its own gravity. And, if the moon reflected the sun's rays in this way, what of the other heavenly bodies? "In the whole universe," said Leonardo, "I do not perceive a body greater or more powerful than the sun, and its light illuminates all the celestial bodies distributed throughout the

Niccolò Machiavelli (1469–1527) was a government official in Florence during the years that the Medici family was out of power (1498–1512). In his famous book The Prince (1513), Machiavelli described how immoral practices—including dishonesty and the murder of rivals—could be justified in the quest for political power.

universe." Even if a man were as big as the Earth, he "would seem like one of the least of the stars which appears but a speck in the universe."

Leonardo no longer believed in the old idea that the Earth was the center of the universe. He saw it as a "speck in the universe," with the sun shining on it and other "stars." This was far from Aristotle's view; it was closer to the **heliocentric** concept of the solar system that Polish astronomer Nicolaus Copernicus would propose four decades later.

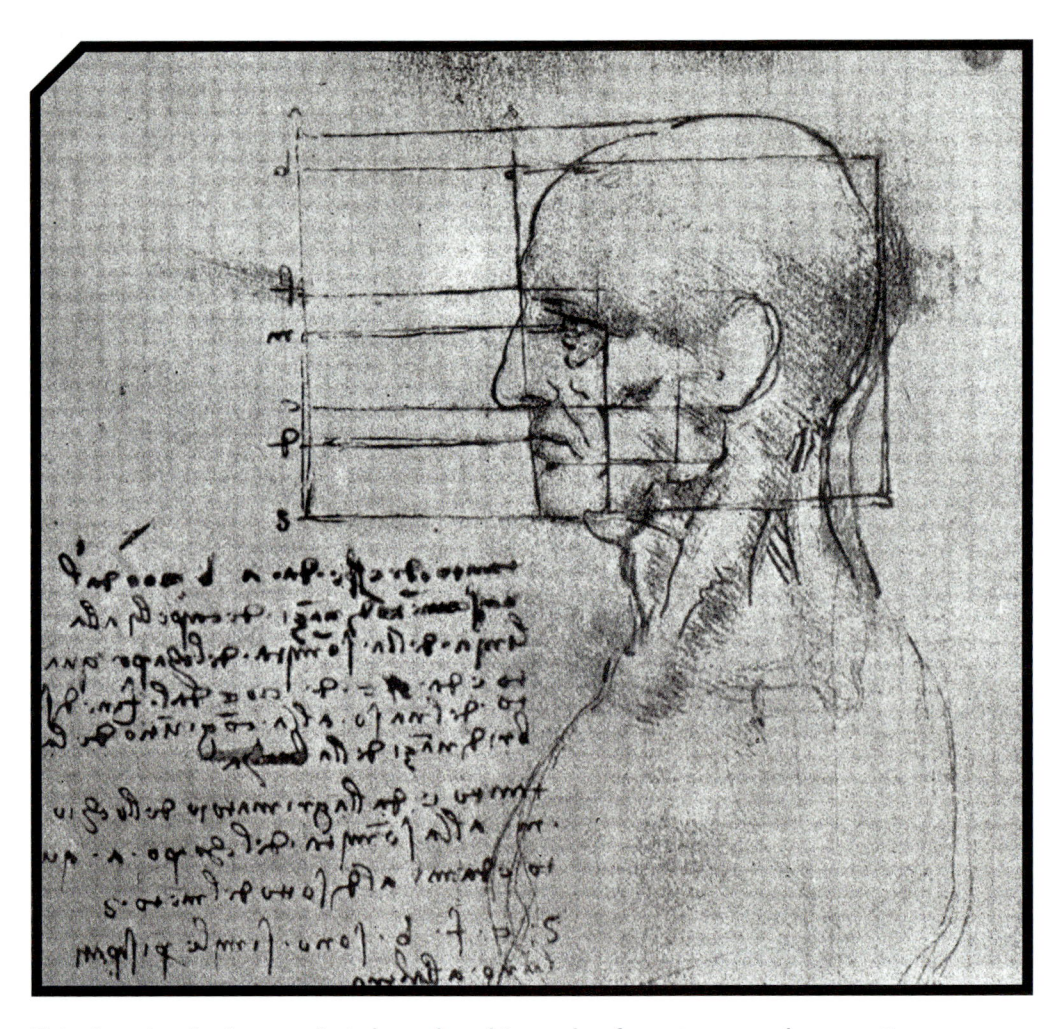

This drawing by Leonardo is based on his study of anatomy and proportions.

Leonardo's return to Florence was not entirely successful. His attempt to paint a fresco in the Palazzo Vecchio was a spectacular failure (for more information, see "Lost Painting in Florence," pp. 52–53). He also failed in his final attempt to get his flying machine to fly. When in 1506 King Louis XII of France asked him to go back to Milan, Leonardo went willingly, with great relief.

Organizing His Thoughts

In 1504, while he was still in Florence, Leonardo's father died without leaving a will. A little later, Leonardo's uncle, Francesco, also died and left Leonardo some property. His brothers were unwilling to let him keep this property because Leonardo was a bastard. This upset Leonardo a great deal and so he took his brothers to court, claiming not only the property left to him by his uncle, Francesco, but a share of his father's property as well. While this dragged on, Leonardo had to leave Milan to visit Florence, where he stayed at the house of his friend, Martelli. Leonardo's notes were in a great muddle and so he used the time to try and get them into order. But even now he began yet another notebook. He started it with the words, "Begun at Florence in the house of Piero di Braccio Martelli, on the 22nd day of March, 1508. This will be a collection without order, made up of many sheets which I have copied here, hoping afterwards to arrange them in order in their proper places according to the subjects of which they treat."

This notebook shows that Leonardo had great difficulty in controlling his thoughts. The first thirty pages contain a fairly neat set of notes on balance, force, gravity, movement and percussion. But then he breaks out into descriptions of experiments on fire in stoves, sunlight on waves, and the movement of paddlewheels in water, etc. Although he did not realize it, Leonardo was about to craft some of the most brilliant research of his life. For by now, he had built up a theory of how the "four powers of nature" worked in the great world ("macrocosm"). He was ready to apply this to the small world (or **microcosm**) of the human body.

At about this time, Leonardo visited an old man in the hospital of Santa Maria Nuova, in Florence. He wrote, "This old man, a few hours before his death, told

LOST PAINTING IN FLORENCE

In 1503, Leonardo was given a contract to create an enormous painting in a government building in Florence, the Palazzo Vecchio. This was to be a fresco—a painting on wet plaster—depicting a famous victory by Florence's army over Milan at Anghiari in 1440. It would appear in an enormous hall where the 500 members of a council that ruled Florence would meet. (After the Medici ruler had been driven out in 1494, a democratic government had been formed in Florence.)

But Leonardo wasn't the only person who would be working on a painting in that room. Another fresco was planned for the opposite wall, to commemorate Florence's 1364 victory over Pisa's troops at Cascina. The artist chosen for this artwork was another famous Florentine: Michelangelo.

Michelangelo was twenty-nine years old in 1503, and many people considered him the primary rival to the fifty-one-year-old Leonardo. Michelangelo had gained fame for his sculpture work in Rome, as well as for a statue of the Biblical hero David that had been installed outside the Palazzo Vecchio. Michelangelo and Leonardo did not like each other, and their artistic styles were very different.

Leonardo worked hard on his painting, *The Battle of Anghiari*, which depicted the heart of that battle. Some of his sketches of mounted soldiers still exist; the faces of these figures reflect Leonardo's opinion of war as "the most bestial of passions." He even invented an elevator-like device that would enable him to easily be raised up to work on the upper part of the wall. Leonardo had experienced trouble with other fresco paintings, such as *The Last Supper*, so he experimented with new techniques and materials. Instead of using water-based paints typical of fresco painting, he tried using oil paints mixed with wax. Unfortunately, this time Leonardo's experiment failed. The paint started to run, so to help it dry faster Leonardo brought in pans containing hot coals that

Dutch artist Peter Paul Reubens drew this detail from Leonardo's painting The Battle of Anghiari. *By the time this drawing was created in 1603, the painting had long been covered over; Reubens may have copied an engraving of the painting, or Leonardo's original cartoon.*

would heat the room. Unfortunately, this made the situation worse. The wax in the paints melted and the colors ran together, destroying the painting. Leonardo could not bring himself to begin the painting all over again, even though this was demanded of him.

Michelangelo was never able to complete his own painting, *The Battle of Cascina*, either. He created a full-sized, detailed cartoon that observers agreed was a masterpiece. But Michelangelo never finished copying the cartoon onto the walls of the Palazzo Vecchio.

Around 1565, the remains of both paintings were covered over by the art historian Giorgio Vasari, who had been hired to redecorate the council hall in the Palazzo Vecchio. Vasari's painting still exists, but some scholars believe that the remains of Leonardo's *Battle of Anghiari* may have been preserved behind it. In 2011, an Italian expert named Maurizio Seracini conducted a high-tech scan of the council hall. He found evidence that Vasari—a great admirer of Leonardo—might have built a wall over *The Battle of Anghiari* before painting his own fresco on the new wall.

To learn more about Leonardo's fascination with anatomy, scan here:

me that he had lived a hundred years, and that he did not feel any bodily ailment other than weakness. And thus while sitting upon a bed in the hospital of Santa Maria Nuova at Florence, without any movement or sign of anything amiss, he passed away from this life. And I made an anatomy in order to ascertain the cause of so sweet a death, and found that it proceeded from weakness through failure of blood and of the artery that feeds the heart and other lower members, which I found to be very dry, shrunk and withered. And the result of this anatomy I wrote down very carefully."

Leonardo saw the human body as a sensitive, moving machine that enclosed the soul. Of the soul he wrote, "whatever this may be, it is a thing divine. Leave it then to dwell in its work at good pleasure …"

Leonardo now planned how he would investigate the parts or "instruments" of the human body. When Leonardo asked a question, he nearly always tried to answer it. Such answers, however, are often to be found far away from the question, in some unexpected corner of another notebook. The first plan of his work in anatomy we know to have been written in about 1489. But the same pages of notes contain entries made in about 1508, nearly twenty years later.

Clearly, he kept his notebooks all those years and took up the subject of anatomy again when he felt the time was ripe.

One plan for the "arrangement of the book" begins, "This work should commence with the conception of man, and should describe the nature of the womb, and how the child inhabits it, how it dwells there, the manner of its quickening and feeding and growth ... and what thing drives it forth from the body of its mother." He then goes on to measure the parts of the body in an infant and compares these with the measurements in a grown man. Obviously, he intended his anatomy to show the body of man from the very beginning to the very end of life, from the infant in the womb, to the death of an old man 100 years old.

Leonardo's drawings of the infant in the womb are probably the most famous of his anatomical drawings. They were made over twenty years after this plan of the book was laid down. At the same time, he was painting his most famous painting, the *Mona Lisa*. Some think that her famous smile shows that she is pregnant.

Another part of this early program of anatomy says, "Represent work with pulling, pushing, carrying, stopping, and supporting, and suchlike things." This part of his plan occupied him over many years. Many sheets contain drawings of little men walking, running, lifting, etc. Often the center of gravity is shown by a line. Movement, in Leonardo's view, was always caused by "unequal distribution of weight around the center of gravity."

Finally, he planned to describe, "the functions of the eye . . . and the other senses." Leonardo made studies of the eye for the whole of his life. They are found scattered in many notebooks. In about 1508, he tried to summarize them in one small book. This contains many experiments on models of the eye and its parts, such as the lens and the **cornea**, and the brave efforts he made to trace the path of light through the eyeball. He found that when light passed through a little hole, like the pupil of the eye, the image was turned upside-down. This is the principle of the *camera obscura*, the forerunner of the photographic camera. Leonardo discovered this, but it led him astray in his studies of the eye, for he could not imagine that the image of an object was thrown on to the back of the eye upside-down. He therefore suggested that the lens in the middle of the eye turned it the right way up again.

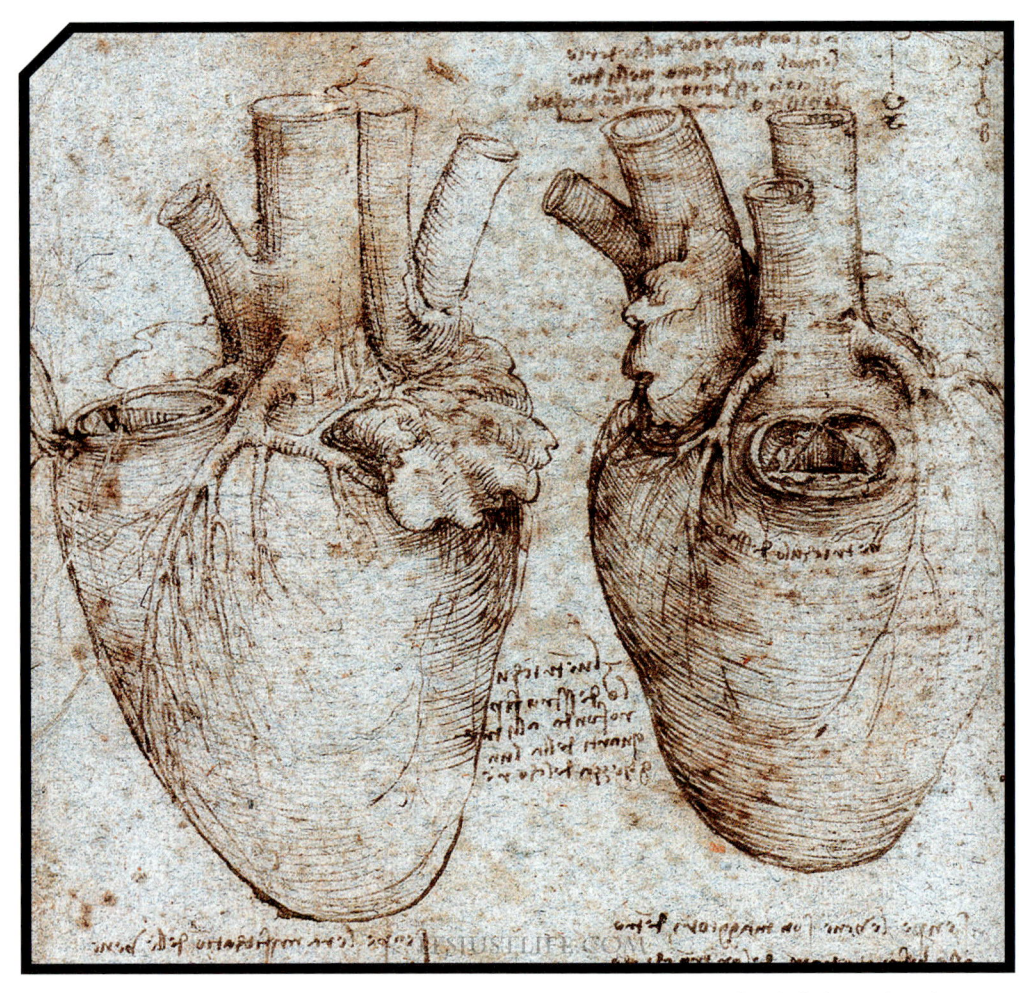

Leonardo's drawings of the human heart. In these drawings both left and right coronary arteries are shown sending their branches to the muscle of the heart. These are followed in detail. At the right margin Leonardo shows the coronary arteries "crowning" the top of the heart. This is how they got their name "coronary."

At the same time, Leonardo was returning to the study of anatomy. In about 1508, he drew up further programs of research. He had now done a great deal of work on the forces of nature. So, he told himself, "Arrange it so that the book of the elements of mechanics with examples shall precede the demonstration of the movement and force of man and other animals." And, "Why Nature cannot give the power of movement to animals without mechanical instruments is shown by me in this book on the movement which Nature has created in animals. For this reason I have drawn up the rules of the four powers of Nature without which nothing through her can give local movement to these animals ..." Then he describes the four powers: movement, weight, force and percussion. He planned to describe not only the anatomy, but the "actions," or physiology, of the organs of the body. He was setting out to show how the "four powers" work in that small world, or "microcosm," of the body, as well as in the large world, or "macrocosm."

Leonardo thought carefully about how he was going to dissect and draw the parts of the human body. "This plan of mine of the human body will be unfolded to you just as though you had the natural man before you," he explained in his notes. Leonardo continued:

> The reason is that if you wish to know the anatomy of man thoroughly you must turn either him or your eye to see him from different directions, from above, below and from the sides . . . It is necessary to have several dissections, three to give full knowledge of the veins and arteries, three for the membranes, three for the nerves, muscles and ligaments, three for the bones and cartilages . . . and three you must have for the female body, and in this there is a great mystery by reason of the womb and its fetus. Thus, in fifteen complete figures you will have set before you the microcosm on the same plan as before me was used by Ptolemy in his cosmography [a famous book on ancient geography]. I shall divide it into parts just as he divided the world into provinces. Then I shall define the function of each part, placing before your eyes knowledge of the whole shape and force of man in so far as he has local movement of his parts.

This was his scheme for illustrating the anatomy and physiology (which he saw as "shape and force") of the whole human body. For each part of the body, he made a separate plan. For example, outlining his plan for the anatomy of the neck, Leonardo said to himself, "You should first show the spine of the neck with its tendons like the mast of a ship with its shrouds outside the head."

Leonardo dissected about thirty bodies altogether. The body of the "Old Man," because it was free from fat, he found the easiest, particularly for the viscera such as the stomach, liver and intestines. Many of his drawings of these parts are actually labeled, "Old Man."

As he dissected and drew, Leonardo was repeatedly overcome with the beauty and wonder of what he was revealing. His pages are scattered with exclamations of admiration. For example, beside a figure of the heart he exclaimed, "Marvelous instrument invented by the supreme Master." And, "With what words O writer, can you with like perfection describe the whole arrangement of what is drawn here?"

In order to discover the true shapes of cavities like those inside the brain and heart, Leonardo used his experience as a sculptor. He injected these organs with wax and made plaster casts. His drawings of the skeleton showed his knowledge of the mechanics of movements and postures. It was Leonardo who showed the true shape of the spine and the tilt of the pelvis for the first time.

The arms and legs gave him a good chance to explain his principles of the lever. Every muscle was dissected to show how it acted to make the bony levers move. Having dissected out a muscle, Leonardo would tug it to show how it worked. In this way, he built up a complete picture of how the limbs and their joints moved. One that really pleased him was the action of the biceps. This muscle, he found, not only bent the arm at the elbow but turned the palm of the hand upward as well. He made a number of special drawings to show how it did this.

When he had worked out how all the muscles in the leg worked, he made a model, putting on to its bones copper wires that ran along what he called the "lines of force" of each muscle.

Most of this anatomical work was done after Leonardo had returned to Milan from Florence. For a while, he led a peaceful life. He would often stay with his friends, the Melzi family, who lived outside Milan at Vaprio on the Adda River. Here, he found a young pupil, Francesco Melzi, a talented artist. Leonardo became "like a father" to Francesco Melzi.

One of the reasons that Leonardo did so much anatomy at this time was that he had also had the good fortune to meet an anatomist. Vasari described this meeting, saying that Leonardo was "aiding and being aided by M. Marcantonio della Torre, a profound philosopher who then professed at Padua

Visitors take photos of Leonardo's Mona Lisa at the Louvre Museum in Paris. Mona Lisa is one of the world's most famous artworks. Leonardo had been hired by a middle class merchant in Florence to paint the portrait of his wife, Lisa del Giocondo, in 1503. However, he was not able to finish the painting due to other commitments. Leonardo took the painting with him when he left Florence for Milan, and continued working on it until a few years before his death.

The Basilica of Saint Mary, one of the largest Roman Catholic churches in Rome, is home to the Leonardo da Vinci Museum. It contains models of many of the military machines he designed, as well as examples of his anatomical drawings and artwork.

WORDS TO UNDERSTAND

alchemy—the primitive stage of chemistry, mainly concerned with changing all metals into the "perfect" metal, gold, and the discovery of the elixir of life.

cambium—a layer of cells in plants or trees from which plant tissues (such as wood) are formed.

concave—a hollow curved surface, like the inside of a sphere.

phyllotaxis—the arrangement of leaves on the stem of a plant or the branch of a tree.

vital spirit—the substance that gives life to people, believed by the ancient Greeks to be located in the left ventricle of the heart.

CHAPTER 5

Rome, City of Disillusion

Leonardo and his little band left for Rome full of hope. The two Medici brothers, Pope Leo and Giuliano de' Medici, promised to turn Rome into a bigger and better Florence. Pope Leo was a typical Renaissance figure—learned, cultured, and fond of the arts, particularly music. He was scornful of mechanical experiment. But Giuliano was different. In some way he sensed the mystery of science. His interest was in **alchemy**. He saw to it that Leonardo was well paid and lodged in luxurious quarters in the palace of the Belvedere, on the top of the Vatican hill. Leonardo was also provided with a laboratory and a workshop with paid assistants. Here, the gardens had been laid out with rare plants from all over the world. There was also the great Vatican library founded by Pope Sixtus IV and a zoo containing strange animals, among them a white elephant. At last Leonardo had the ideal place for his work.

Previously, Leonardo had rejected alchemy. But now, probably because of Giuliano's interests, he began to look at the subject in his own way. When, in the past, he had made his own paints, he had made improved distilling flasks that could be cooled down more easily. He used these in his laboratory in Rome with substances that he called Venus, Mercury and Jupiter—the alchemists' names for copper, mercury, and tin.

But when it came to the distillation of plant juices to find an improved varnish for his pictures, his experiments did him no good. Pope Leo thought this highly amusing. Here was Leonardo busy preparing the varnish before he had even begun to paint a picture. "Alas," he exclaimed, "this man will never get anything done, for he is thinking about the end before he begins." This spiteful little joke shows the difference between the Pope and Leonardo. It also explains why Leonardo did not paint any pictures while he was in Rome.

Perhaps a little pig-headedly, Leonardo turned instead to the invention of metal screws which, until then, had never been used. He produced a screw-cutting machine that remained in use until the twentieth century. This machine was the result of many past studies on the screw that had been part of his work on the helicopter and propeller.

Trouble in Rome

At about this time, Leonardo had trouble in his workshop from his assistant, a German named Georgio. This man asked for an increase in wages, and when Leonardo refused, Georgio went on strike. Leonardo was making **concave** mirrors at this time, so that he could view a greatly magnified image of the moon or of the other "stars." The mirrors were so big that they were to be mounted and moved out into the Belvedere Gardens. It seems that this was Leonardo's secret project. He was angry when he found out that Georgio had been telling his secrets to a mirror maker, Giovanni delgi Specchi, who was paying for

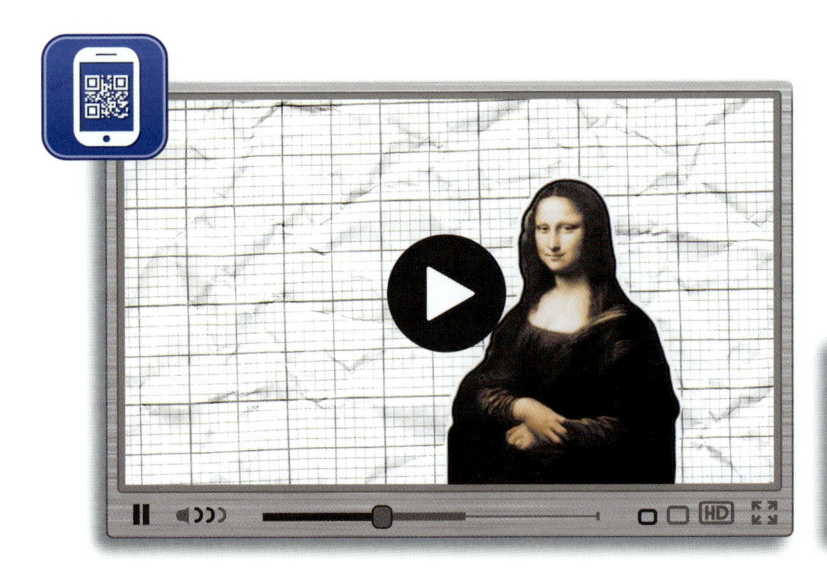

Scan here to see a short video about Leonardo's masterpiece, Mona Lisa:

the information. When he was discovered, the mirror maker reported Leonardo to the Pope for performing anatomical dissections at the hospital. The Pope forbade Leonardo to continue with the studies of human corpses. Undaunted, Leonardo acquired the hearts of cattle from a slaughterhouse and began to study the anatomy of the heart very carefully.

Many pages of Leonardo's notebooks are filled with the results of these dissections. They were among the last dissections that he did, and led him to disagree completely with old ideas about what the heart was, and how it worked. These ideas had come from Aristotle and Galen, who thought the heart was a center of **vital spirit** and emotional feeling. These ideas persist today, as when people refer to someone as "hard-hearted," or complain about those who make "half-hearted" efforts.

Pope Leo X (1475–1521) was the son of Milan's former ruler, Lorenzo de' Medici. He was elected pope in 1513, and held the office until his death in 1521. He was a patron of the arts, hiring Renaissance artists to decorate church buildings throughout Rome.

Aristotle, Galen, and other ancient thinkers believed that the heart generated heat for the body. This heat, they thought, flowed out through the arteries with the "vital spirit." In a similar way, food absorbed from the stomach was thought to pass through the liver, where it was turned into blood and then sent as

This illuminated manuscript from the fifteenth century depicts Galen of Pergamon and his assistant preparing medicine. Galen (129–c. 216 CE) was a Greek-speaking physician who lived in the Roman Empire. His writings on anatomy and medicine dominated Western science until the sixteenth century, when the anatomical studies of Leonardo and others provided new insights into the functions and operations of the human body.

nourishment to all parts of the body through the veins. Some blood passed into one of the two chambers (ventricles) of the heart. A little of this blood passed from the right ventricle to the left ventricle through the wall, or septum, between them. The heart was thought to be too "noble" to be just muscle. It was special. Its main job was to expand and suck in air from the lungs. From this air the "vital spirits " were made in the left ventricle and then sent out to the rest of the body through the arteries.

Leonardo felt that there was a great deal wrong with these ideas. First, he announced that the heart was a muscle, and like other muscles, it was supplied by arteries, veins, and nerves. Like other muscles, it contracted, and this contraction "percussed" the blood that it contained into the arteries. He claimed that the heart was made up of four, not two, chambers. The two upper chambers

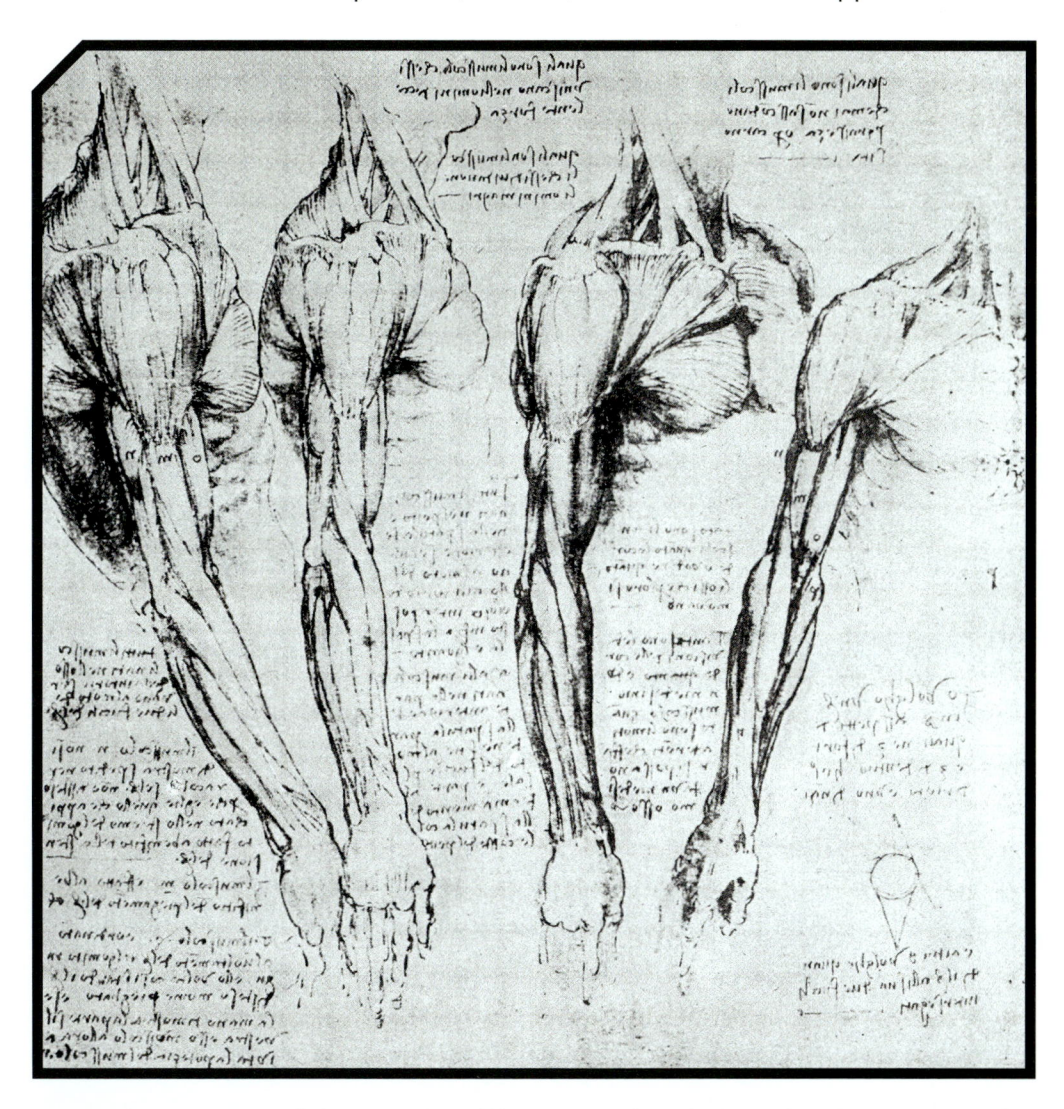

Leonardo's drawing of the muscles of the arm and neck, based on his anatomical studies.

Statue of Leonardo in the Villa Borghese Gardens, Rome.

he called the "atria," and the two lower chambers, the "ventricles." When the heart beats, said Leonardo, the atria contract first and force the blood they contain into the ventricles. Then the ventricles contract and force their blood into the pulmonary artery and aorta which take the blood around the body.

So far, he was completely right. But the next part of his theory was wrong. He thought that not all the blood in the ventricles went into the arteries—only part of it. Some, Leonardo said, went back into the atria before the valves between them closed. This blood, he thought, expanded the atria, so that it was then able to receive more blood from the liver. Another contraction of the atria once again forced this blood into the ventricles.

Why did Leonardo suggest this "to-and-fro" movement of blood between the atria and ventricles? It was because he accepted the ancient belief that the heart was the source of body heat, as well as the source of power for circulating blood around the body. "Heat," he wrote, "is produced by the movement of the heart. This manifests itself because in proportion as the heart moves more quickly the heat increases. This is shown by the pulse of those suffering from fever." Thus, the flow of blood between the atria and ventricles would, in his view, produce friction between the blood and walls of the heart. From this friction, heat would be produced for the body. Leonardo suggested testing his theory by a trial with churning milk. If he was right, the movement of the milk against the sides of the churn would produce heat.

In the slaughterhouse, Leonardo watched pigs being killed by having skewers thrust into their hearts. There, he studied the movements of the dying pigs' hearts. He saw that the beat of the heart coincided with the movement of blood from the ventricles into the main arteries by "percussion." He was very interested in the movement of blood into the aorta, and made a glass model of this part of the heart so that he could look at it more closely.

In 1514, Leonardo was given other work to do. Pope Leo was a keen huntsman. But he was afraid of the diseases, particularly malaria, that were common in the marshy lands around Rome. The Pope sent Leonardo out of Rome to an area along the coast known as the Pontine marshes, and instructed Leonardo to work out a plan for draining the marshland. This plan was drawn by Leonardo on a map of the region. He suggested digging a canal at a small town called Badino, so the marsh waters could be drained into the Martino River. Later in the century, Leonardo's plan was utilized by an engineer, Giovanni Scotto, who succeeded in draining the area around Badino. The rest of the Pontine marshes were successfully drained in the 1930s by a network of canals that followed and improved on Leonardo's plan.

Leonardo's trips in the countryside around Rome and his easy access to the Belvedere Gardens had renewed his early interest in plants. At once, he saw a similarity between the movement of sap in a plant and the movement of blood in an animal. "The same cause," he wrote, "moves water through the veins of the earth as moves blood in the human species . . . In the same way water rises from the low roots of the vine to its lofty top and falling on the primal roots mounts anew."

When he wrote these words, he thought that it was heat that caused blood and sap to move. It was only in these last years, as we have seen, that he realized that blood was pumped around the body of animals by the beating of the heart.

Leonardo observed that the rising sap of spring made the "thickness" of trees "between the **cambium** and the wood of the tree." He was the first to notice that growth took place in the cambium. He went on to note that each year's wood formed a ring, and that the age of trees could be found out by counting the number of rings of annual growth. This observation made him the founder of the study of "dendrochronology" by which wood can be dated. In recent years, this has been much used for dating paintings on wood—something that would have pleased Leonardo a great deal.

Leonardo's studies on the pattern of branch and leaf formation in plants were the first to reveal the basic principles of what is called **phyllotaxis** (leaf arrangement).

"All flowers that see the sun mature their seed, and not the others," wrote Leonardo. He compared what he saw in seeds with his studies of the infant in the womb. "All seeds have an umbilical cord which breaks when the seed is ripe; and in like manner they have matrix [uterus] and secundina [membranes] as is shown in seeds that grow in pods."

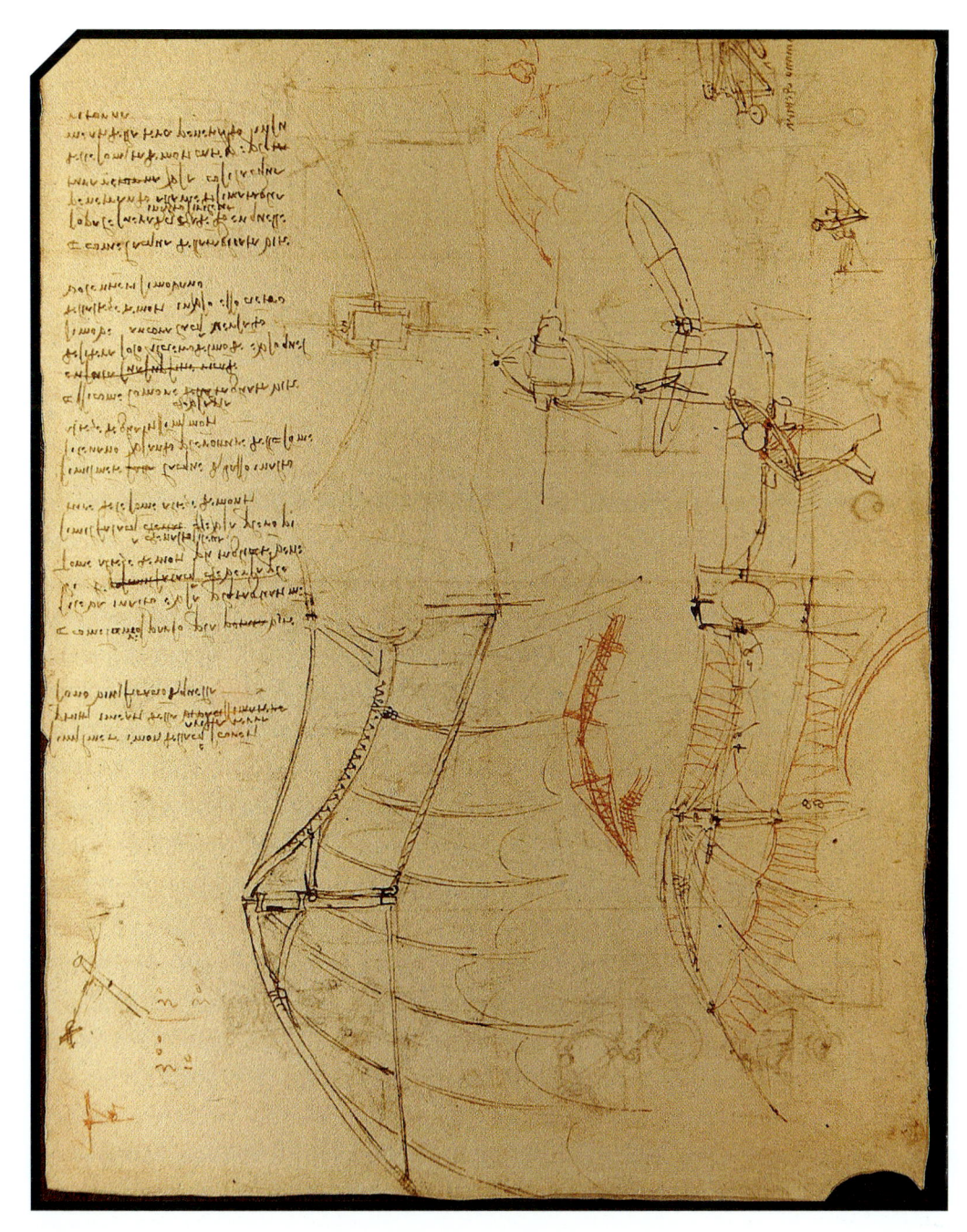

Leonardo's sketches for a flying machine. Leonardo's efforts were concentrated on imitating the flight of birds and were unsuccessful.

During these unhappy years in Rome, Leonardo's health began to fail. We know this from a letter he wrote to his patron, Giuliano de' Medici, who was seriously ill with tuberculosis. Leonardo wrote, "So greatly did I rejoice, most illustrious Lord, at your much wished for restoration to health that my own malady almost left me."

When Giuliano de' Medici died in March 1516, Leonardo was left lonely and neglected in Rome. His world was coming to an end. It was probably a feeling of doom that led him to make a series of drawings of the powers of nature destroying the world. At the same time, he wrote two essays to accompany the drawings, called *Descriptions of the Deluge*. One of these essays describes the human grief and despair at this awful event. The other describes the event in terms of Leonardo's physics of the "four powers." Both the drawings and the descriptions are based on Leonardo's scientific work on the effects of stones thrown into a pond. One, for example, shows the "percussion" of a vast volcanic explosion, with its blast waves spreading out in concentric rings.

In the summer of 1516, Leonardo went with Pope Leo to Bologna. There he met the young, newly crowned French king Francis I. Leonardo accompanied him back to France, to Amboise on the banks of the river Loire.

TEXT-DEPENDENT QUESTIONS

1. Where did Leonardo live during his time in Rome?
2. How did Leonardo develop his ideas about the working of the human heart?
3. What was Leonardo's plan for the Pontine marshes?
4. What inspired Leonardo to write *Descriptions of the Deluge*?

RESEARCH PROJECT

Using your school library or the internet, research the history of Rome. Why was this city so important in European history during the fifteenth and sixteenth centuries? What was life like in Rome at the time Leonardo was there? Write a two-page report and share it with your class.

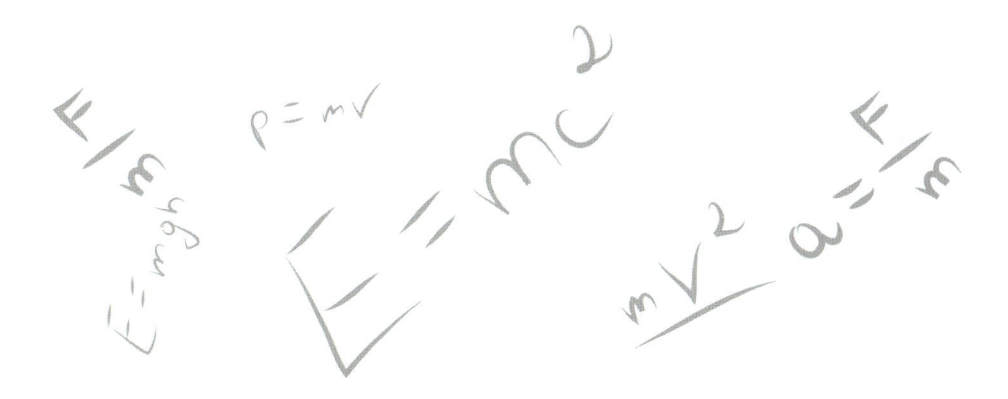

The castle of King Francis at Amboise, in the Loire River valley, where Leonardo spent his final years.

WORDS TO UNDERSTAND

cardinal—a leading dignitary of the Roman Catholic Church.

treatise—a written work that deals formally and systematically with a subject.

vulgar—in Renaissance Europe, this word was used to describe the common language used by people every day, as opposed to Latin, the language of scholarship and law.

CHAPTER 6
Final Years in France

When Leonardo reached Amboise, he was a sick man. King Francis lodged him in a pleasant house called Cloux near his own castle. There, Leonardo again tried to get his scientific observations and experiments into some kind of order. Once more, he failed.

While in Amboise, he painted a mysterious picture of the young Saint John. This figure seemed to have some of the features of a man and some of a woman. Many people have guessed what Leonardo was trying to say in this painting. Perhaps, this was his ideal human being—a person who had the virtues of a man and a woman at the same time. This was his last painting and it was very different from his first. *St. Jerome* clearly shows Leonardo's mastery of anatomy. In *St. John*, Leonardo's great anatomical knowledge is hidden.

In October 1517, an Italian **cardinal** named Luigi d'Aragona saw this and other paintings in Leonardo's house at Amboise. His secretary, Antonio de Beatis, made a note of the meeting. He described Leonardo as "over seventy" when he was actually only sixty-four. Leonardo probably looked older than he really was because he had suffered from a stroke and was left with a crippled right hand. The secretary added to his notes, "This gentleman has written a **treatise** on anatomy showing by illustrations the limbs, muscles, nerves, vessels, joints, intestines, and whatever else is to discuss in the bodies of men and women, in a way that has never yet been done by anyone else. All this we have seen with our own eyes; and he said he had dissected more than thirty bodies, both of men and women of all ages. He has also written of the nature of water, and of diverse machines, and of other matters which he

Francis I, king of France from 1515 to 1547, was a patron of Renaissance art. He invited many Italian artists to work on decorating royal castles in France, including Leonardo. During his rule, Francis also waged a series of wars against Italian city-states such as Florence and Milan, continuing the aggressive policies of previous French rulers.

has set down in an endless number of volumes, all in the **vulgar** tongue, which if they be published will be profitable and delightful." But, by this time, Leonardo thought that they would never be published.

In Amboise, King Francis admired him and called him "a great philosopher." He also interrupted him with daily visits, with plans for festivals and plays, just as Ludovico Sforza had done before him. Leonardo made yet another plan for a palace, this time for rebuilding the castle at Amboise. In it he included new safety and sanitary devices. Rooms that were to be used for crowded festivities and balls were all to be on the ground floor, because, "I have seen many roofs collapse and bury numbers of dead." Timber work was to be bricked in to prevent fire. Washrooms with primitive toilets were to be built in a row, with ventilating shafts, and each room was to have a door that closed automatically. A lake was to be made behind the castle for water jousting, an original touch that greatly impressed the king.

At Romorantin, a lonely place, Leonardo played what he called "Geometrical Games." This was the science of "things possible." He planned the shapes of

During his rule over France, King Francis I renovated and improved a castle at Blois, in the Loire Valley. Part of the new construction included a magnificent spiral staircase, ornamented with fine sculptures, which overlooked the castle's central courtyard. The staircase still exists. Due to its beauty and its left-handed spiral, many experts believe that Leonardo planned this architectural feature. However, there is no definitive proof that he did.

Leonardo on his deathbed at Cloux in 1519, with King Francis I and members of the royal household in attendance.

parts that could be used to make walls, floors, and roofs, so that when they were fitted together, they made houses. This was the beginning of prefabricated buildings.

He studied the Loire River—the movements of its water, its bends and depths and shallows. Once more he told, as he had in Milan and Florence, of the social benefits that canals and dams would bring: "If the effluent of the Loire were turned with its muddy waters into the river of Romorantin this would fatten the land that it would water, and would render the country fertile to supply food for the inhabitants, and would make a navigable channel for merchant shipping."

Leonardo's final surviving notebook entry was the touching, "June 24, 1518, Saint John's Day, at Amboise, in the palazzo of Cloux; I shall go on."

Within year, on May 2, 1519, Leonardo was dead. The only people who followed his funeral were a few servants and village people paid seventy sous each to carry torches. Even after death, his body suffered misfortune. During the French Revolution, the church in which he was buried was destroyed. The tombs were broken into so that robbers could steal their lead, and the bones within

An advertisement at the New York headquarters of the auction house Christie's promotes the sale of a Leonardo da Vinci painting of Jesus, titled Salvator Mundi ("Savior of the World"). The long-lost painting was rediscovered in 2005, and experts spent six years restoring the artwork and verifying that it was indeed Leonardo's work. In November 2017, Salvator Mundi sold at auction for more than $450 million, the highest amount ever paid for a painting.

were scattered. These were later collected and put into a common burial place. Leonardo's bones were presumably among them.

Leonardo's Legacy

Leonardo da Vinci was a pioneer of creative science. He saw that art and science are closely linked, each giving something to the other. For Leonardo, science without art was sterile; and art without science was absurd. Together, the two could make man a creator, a small model of God. Just as God created the great world of nature, man could create his own world of "inventions"—machines that were unknown in nature, but based on observations of nature.

Leonardo knew the dangers of the powers of invention. "I know," he wrote, "that there are numberless people who, to satisfy their lusts, would destroy God and the whole universe." Yet, he insisted that, "Man does not differ from animals except in what is accidental, and in this he shows that he is a divine thing; for where Nature finishes the production of her forms and shapes there man begins, with the assistance of Nature, to make an infinity of forms."

Leonardo had never been able to organize his notes and discoveries during his lifetime, and no one succeeded in doing this after his death either. Leonardo left all the manuscripts that he had taken to France to a devoted pupil, Francesco Melzi (1491–1570). Melzi brought them back to his home at Vaprio, near Milan. Over the years, some people were permitted to see them. For example, it is clear that Vasari had seen the anatomical drawings before writing his life of Leonardo da Vinci. Some took pages of the manuscripts away with them, but Melzi preserved most of them carefully until his own death. He pieced together the

Opposite page: Francesco Melzi's portrait of the aged Leonardo. Melzi was Leonardo's student and assistant from 1505 until Leonardo's death in 1519. They had a very close relationship, which Leonardo compared to a father and son.

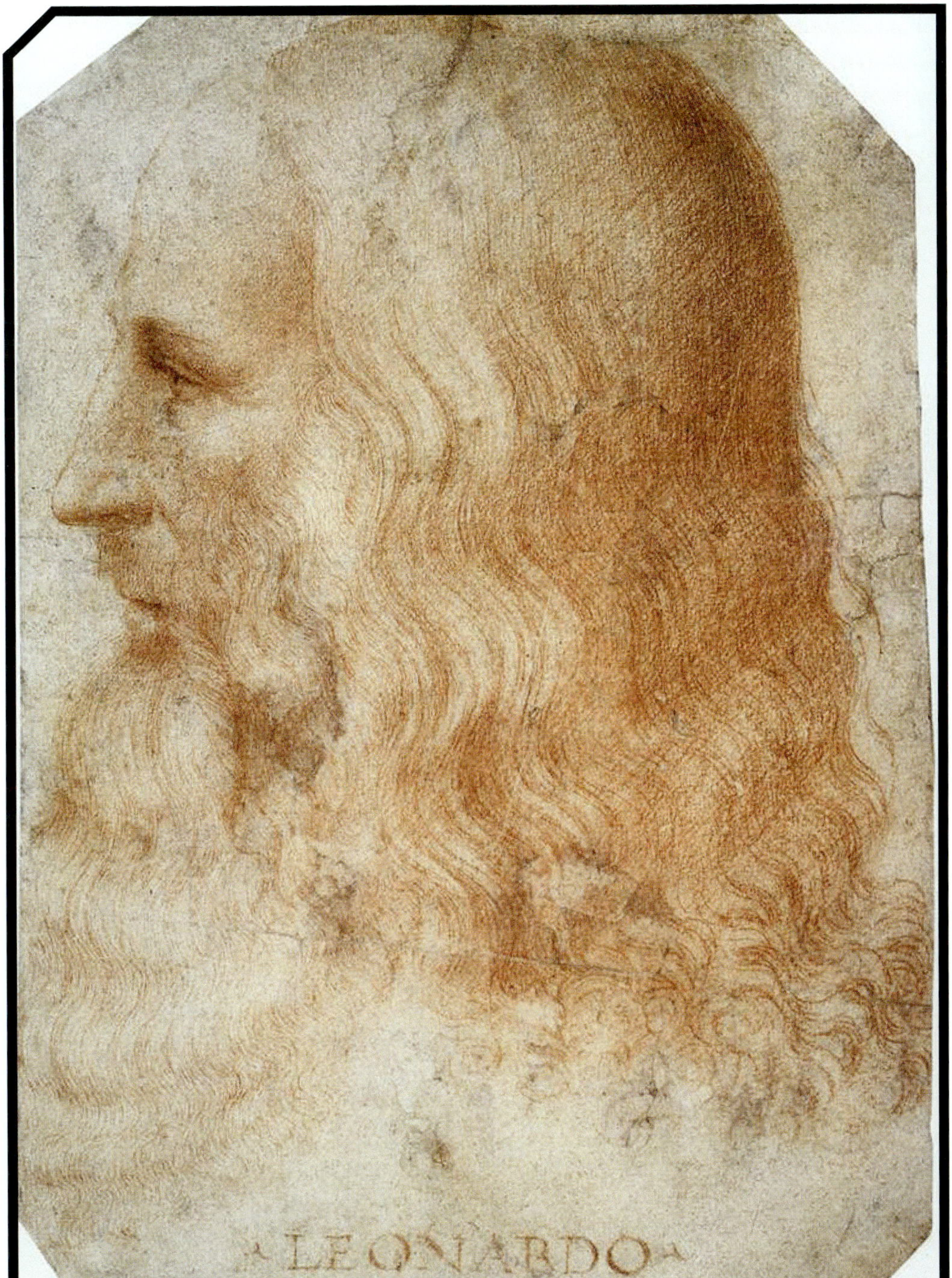
LEONARDO

Scan here to learn more about Leonardo's obsession with flight:

passages about painting. These extracts make up the only book published under Leonardo's name, *The Treatise on Painting* (1651).

After Melzi's death in 1570, the manuscripts were neglected by his son, who put them all in his attic. Over time, the family gave away or sold individual pages. Eventually, an Italian sculptor named Pompeo Leoni collected as many pages as he could find, binding them into several large books called "codices." Today, Leonardo's designs for inventions, his notes on anatomy and science, his architectural designs and plans for unfinished works, and other writings are scattered in museums and libraries across the world.

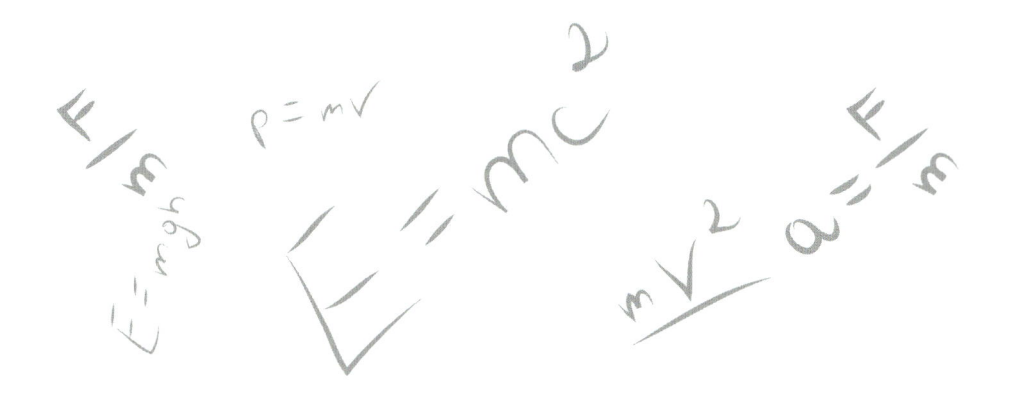

TEXT-DEPENDENT QUESTIONS

1. Where did Leonardo live while he was in France?
2. What did Leonardo do while he was living in France?
3. What pupil inherited Leonardo's manuscripts? What happened to them?

RESEARCH PROJECT

Visit the website http://www.treatiseonpainting.org/intro.html to learn more about the *Treatise on Painting* compiled by Leonardo's pupil Francesco Melzi and eventually printed more than eighty years after Melzi's death.

Chronology

1452
Leonardo is born on April 15.

1466
Leonardo moves into Verrocchio's workshop.

1469
Lorenzo de' Medici comes to power in Florence. Ser Piero da Vinci, Leonardo's father, moves to Florence.

1472
Leonardo is enrolled into the Company of Painters.

1473
Leonardo's first dated drawing, a landscape, shows his interest in geology.

1476
Leonardo is accused of homosexuality, but later acquitted.

1481
Leonardo starts to paint *St. Jerome* and *The Adoration of the Magi*. He never finishes them. Leonardo writes to Ludovico Sforza.

1483
Receives contract for the *Virgin of the Rocks*, after moving from Florence to Milan during the previous year.

1487
The Trivulziano Codex commenced. In it, Leonardo's first scientific ideas appear. Many pages are devoted to lists of words. Plans for waterways and satellite cities made.

Statue of Leonardo da Vinci in the Piazza della Scala, Milan.

1488–89
Manuscript B. This contains some of Leonardo's most brilliant architectural drawings, including plans of cities and fortifications. His earliest plans for constructing a flying machine, with research into the mechanics of flight, are here.

1489
Leonardo begins his anatomical research on the human and the horse.

1490
Leonardo advises on the cathedral at Pavia. Starts work on the statue of Duke Francesco on horseback.

1490–92

Manuscript A written. This was his first important scientific notebook containing a mixture of notes on weight, geometry, ballistics, optics, hydraulics, percussion, painting, and perspective. Manuscript C, a notebook mostly on light and shade, written. Volume III of the Codex Forster—a notebook Leonardo carried with him—also written at this time. It contains notes on architecture, knots, horses, geometry, and studies of balance.

1493

The model of the Sforza monument erected.

1496

Luca Pacioli, the mathematician, comes to Milan and befriends Leonardo. Codex Madrid I. A systematic study of the "Elements of Mechanics."

1497

The Last Supper completed. Manuscript H completed. It contains many animal fables, prophecies, notes on plants, warfare, and Latin grammar. Manuscript M started. It shows the mathematical influence of Luca Pacioli, being full of geometry, mechanics, and studies of the "four powers." Manuscript I also contains notes on Latin grammar and hydraulics.

1499

The French occupy Milan. Leonardo leaves Milan for Venice.

1500

French bowmen use the Sforza monument for target practice. Leonardo returns to Florence, where he studies geometry once more with Luca Pacioli.

1501

The Cartoon of St. Anne exhibited.

1502

Leonardo travels with Cesare Borgia. Meets Machiavelli. Begins Manuscript L, which contains notes on bird flight, as well as designs for fortresses.

1503
Leonardo returns to Florence. Advises on the diversion of the river Arno behind Pisa. Concentrates on the formations of the earth, geology.

1504
Ser Piero, Leonardo's father, dies without leaving a will. The fresco painting *Battle of Anghiari* is ruined. Begins painting the *Mona Lisa*. Begins the Madrid Codex II, a notebook containing a number of maps, a list of books in Leonardo's library, and notes on birds and geometry.

1505
Final attempt at flight of his "bird" ends in failure. Keeps notebook on the flight of birds, as well as Codex Forster I, on geometry and mechanics.

1506
Leonardo goes back to Milan, but visits Florence to pursue a lawsuit against his brothers over his inheritance from his father and uncle. Begins the Codex Leicester, a volume almost entirely devoted to studies of the movement and measurement of water in relation to the formation of the earth.

1508
Starts trying to arrange his notes while in Florence. This new notebook is now known as the Codex Arundel. Performs anatomical dissection of the "Old Man" in the hospital of Santa Maria Nuova, Florence. Keeps a special notebook on the eye, Manuscript D. Another set of writings, known as Manuscript F, includes notes on the eye, along with observations about water and astronomy.

1509–10
Concentrates on anatomy in Milan, working with Marcantonio della Torre. A pocket notebook, Manuscript K, contains notes on rivers, horses, geometry, and the movements of the elements by the "powers."

1512
The French leave Milan.

1513
Leonardo leaves Milan for Rome with Francesco Melzi and others. Leonardo composes Manuscript G on painting, especially landscapes and botany. Manuscript E includes notes on the mechanics of the "powers," particularly in relation to the flight of birds.

1514
While in Rome, studies chemistry, botany, concave mirrors, and anatomy of the heart. Plans the drainage of the Pontine marshes. Makes drawings for *The Deluge*. First signs of declining health.

1516
Leonardo goes to France. Paints *St. John*.

1517
Studies the Loire River. Designs a palace at Romorantin. Visited by Cardinal Luigi d'Aragona.

1518
Leonardo's last note: "I shall go on."

1519
Dies on May 2.

Note: the Codex Atlanticus, so-named because it is so large, contains a mass of notes—mostly on mechanics—that date from 1480 to 1518. It contains about 1,000 pages. The Codex Arundel, Leonardo's attempted revision, covers an almost equally wide range of subjects and time. It contains about 1,200 rather smaller pages. Despite some relatively recent discoveries, most experts believe that we possess only about one-third of Leonardo's notes.

Further Reading

Atalay, Bulent, and Keith Wamsley. *Leonardo's Universe: the Renaissance World of Leonardo da Vinci.* Washington, D.C.: National Geographic, 2009.

Bauer, Susan Wise. *The Story of Western Science: From the Writings of Aristotle to the Big Bang Theory.* New York: W. W. Norton, 2015.

Bynum, William. *A Little History of Science.* New Haven, Conn.: Yale University Press, 2012.

Capra, Fritjof. *The Science of Leonardo: Inside the Mind of the Great Genius of the Renaissance.* New York: Anchor Books, 2007.

Isaacson, Walter. *Leonardo da Vinci.* New York: Simon & Schuster, 2017.

Klein, Stefan. *Leonardo's Legacy: How da Vinci Re-imagined the World.* Trans. by Shelley Frisch. Cambridge, Mass.: Da Capo Press, 2010.

Nicholl, Charles. *Leonardo da Vinci: Flights of the Mind.* New York: Viking, 2004.

Suh, H. Anna, ed. *Leonardo's Notebooks: Writing and Art of the Great Master.* New York: Black Dog & Leventhal Publishers, 2014.

Internet Resources

www.leonardoda-vinci.org

Reproductions of all of Leonardo da Vinci's paintings, as well as information on his life, can be found at this website.

www.bl.uk/manuscripts/Viewer.aspx?ref=arundel_ms_263_f001r

In 2013 the British Library digitized the entire Arundel Codex, a collection of papers written in Italian by Leonardo, so that anyone can page through and view his illustrations and notes.

www.mos.org/leonardo/node/1

The Boston Museum of Science provides this website that teaches students about Leonardo's brilliant and imaginative mind, as well as the art, inventions, and discoveries that he made.

www.pbs.org/wgbh/nova

The website of NOVA, a science series that airs on PBS. The series produces in-depth science programming on a variety of topics, from the latest breakthroughs in technology to the deepest mysteries of the natural world.

www.biology4kids.com/files/studies_scimethod.html

A simple explanation of the scientific method is available at this website for young people.

www.livescience.com

The website Live Science is regularly updated with articles on scientific topics and new developments or discoveries.

Series Glossary of Key Terms

anomaly—something that differs from the expectations generated by an established scientific idea. Anomalous observations may inspire scientists to reconsider, modify, or come up with alternatives to an accepted theory or hypothesis.

evidence—test results and/or observations that may either help support or help refute a scientific idea. In general, raw data are considered evidence only once they have been interpreted in a way that reflects on the accuracy of a scientific idea.

experiment—a scientific test that involves manipulating some factor or factors in a system in order to see how those changes affect the outcome or behavior of the system.

hypothesis—a proposed explanation for a fairly narrow set of phenomena, usually based on prior experience, scientific background knowledge, preliminary observations, and logic.

natural world—all the components of the physical universe, as well as the natural forces at work on those things.

objective—to consider and represent facts without being influenced by biases, opinions, or emotions. Scientists strive to be objective, not subjective, in their reasoning about scientific issues.

observe—to note, record, or attend to a result, occurrence, or phenomenon.

science—knowledge of the natural world, as well as the process through which that knowledge is built through testing ideas with evidence gathered from the natural world.

subjective—referring to something that is influenced by biases, opinions, and/or emotions. Scientists strive to be objective, not subjective, in their reasoning about scientific issues.

test—an observation or experiment that could provide evidence regarding the accuracy of a scientific idea. Testing involves figuring out what one would expect to observe if an idea were correct and comparing that expectation to what one actually observes.

theory—a broad, natural explanation for a wide range of phenomena in science. Theories are concise, coherent, systematic, predictive, and broadly applicable, often integrating and generalizing many hypotheses. Theories accepted by the scientific community are generally strongly supported by many different lines of evidence. However, theories may be modified or overturned as new evidence is discovered.

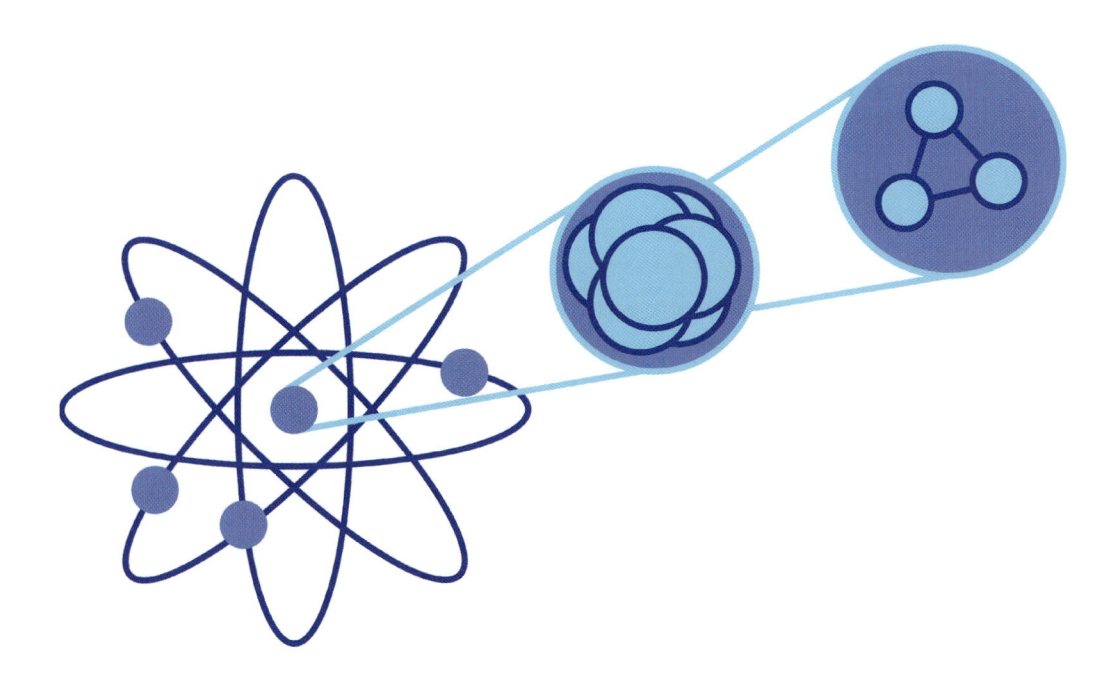

Index

A

accidental movement, 32, 37
Adoration of the Magi, 16, 18
air current (on flight), 26
air, movement of, 42
Alberti, Leon Battista, 14
Albiera, Donna (Ser Piero da Vinci's wife), 9
alchemy, 62, 63
Alexander VI (Roman Catholic Pope), 47
algebra, 40–41
Amboise (France), 75, 76
anatomical drawings, 14
anatomy, 6, 12, 13
anatomy (art), 14, 15, 23, 28, 50, 54(QR code), 57, 75
ancient writings (Greek and Roman), 9
Annunciation, 6, 14
apothecary, 6, 11
Archimedes, 25, 27, 33, 34
architecture, 7, 18, 26, 28
Architronito (steam-powered gun), 25
Aristotle, 16, 33, 37, 38, 50, 65
astronomy, 13
atria, 69

B

ball bearing, 39
Basilica of Saint Mary, 62
Battle of Anghiari, 52, 53
Battle of Cascina (Michelangelo), 53
Biblical Gospel of John, 30
blood, movement of, 69, 70
bodies of birds, study of, 25–26
bookkeeping, 40–41
Borgia, Caesar, 47–48
Bramante, 28
breech-loading mechanism, 25
Brunelleschi, Filippo, 14
Byzantine Empire (Eastern Roman Empire), 9

C

cambium, 62, 70
canals, 27–28, 42, 48, 70, 78
cannon barrels, 24, 25
cardinal, 74, 75
cartoon, 44, 45, 46–47, 53
Cathedral dome (Florentine), 14
Chapel of the Immaculate Conception, 22
Company of Painters (1472), 14
concave, 62, 64
condottieri (hired soliders), 7
confraternity, 20, 22
Constantinople (Istanbul), 8, 9
convection current, 20, 25
Convent of Santa Maria delle Grazie, 29, 30
Copernicus, Nicolaus, 50
cornea, 44
cranes, flight of, 26
crossbow, 17

D

d'Aragona, Luigi, 75
da Vinci, Caterina (mother), 8–9
da Vinci, Francesco (uncle), 9, 51
da Vinci, Leonardo
  animals, interest in, 10, 16, 25
  birth, family history and death, 7, 8–9, 21, 23, 25, 51, 74, 75, 79–80
  botanical research, 14
  character, 15–16, 21
  education, 10, 11
  inventor, 18, 21, 25–26, 40, 42, 80
  language, struggle with, 8, 10, 23, 38
  painting, 14–15, 20, 21, 22–23, 30, 59, 75
  portraits, 12, 44, 68, 78, 80–81, 85
  principles, search of, 33
  quotes, 10, 15, 18, 23, 26, 28, 30, 32, 33, 35, 37
  scientist, 21, 33, 42
  sexuality, 14
da Vinci, Ser Piero (father), 8, 9, 10, 11–12, 45, 51
de Predis, Ambrogio, 22
de' Medici, Cosimo, 8
de' Medici, Giuliano, 63, 72
de' Medici, Lorenzo, 16, 60, 65
de' Medici, Piero, 8
de' Medici, Pope Leo, 63, 72
del Giocondo, Lisa, 59
della Torre, M. Marcantonio, 58, 60
dendrochronology, 70
Descriptions of the Deluge (essay), 72

di Giorgio, Francesco, 27
di Verrocchio, Andrea, 11, 12, 13, 14, 16, 18
dissection, 57–58, 64–65
dynamic forces (movement), 37

E
Earth (terrestrial machine), 33, 37, 47, 50
Eastern Roman Empire (Byzantine Empire), 9
Elements (Euclid), 35
Euclid, 33, 35, 37
experiment, description of, 42
exploded view (illustration), 27
eye, 28, 33, 36, 55

F
Ficino, Marsilio, 8, 16
flight, 82 (QR code)
Florence, 7–8, 13, 14, 16, 18, 21, 23, 48
flying machines, 25, 51, 71
forces of nature, 56–57
Francis I (King), 72, 74, 76, 77, 78
friction, coefficient of, 39

G
Galen of Pergamon, 13, 60, 65, 66
Galileo, 35
Geometrical Games, 76, 78
geometrical pattern, 37
geometry, 30, 32, 40–41, 45, 47
Georgio (assistant to da Vinci), 64
glass vessels, 42
God, 33, 80
Greek (language), 8, 10, 38
guild, 6, 11
Guild of Apothecaries and Doctors, 11
gunpowder, 7

H
Halley's Comet, 13
heart (human), 56, 65–67, 69
helicopter, 25, 64
heliocentric, 44, 50
homosexuality, 14
horse, 29–30
human anatomical research, 29
human knowledge, 12
human larynx, 23

human movement, study of, 15, 57
hydraulics, 18

I
Il Fanfoia (Melzi, Francesco), 58, 60, 80, 82
Il Magnifico (the Magnificent), 8
Immaculate Conception, 22
impetus, 32, 38
inertia, 39
instruments of sound, 23
Istanbul (Constantinople), 8, 9
Italian (language), 23
Italian peninsula, 17

J
Jesus Christ, 30
Judas (apostle), 30
Julius II (Roman Catholic Pope), 48, 60

L
language, 8, 10, 23, 38
Last Supper (1495), 29, 52
Latin (language), 10, 23, 38
Leo X (Pope), 65
Leonardo da Vinci Museum, 62
Leoni, Pompeo, 82
Lepanto (1499), 45
light, 22, 25, 34, 35
light, law of, 34, 48
light, physics of, 14
light, wave theory of, 37
lion, 10
lock, 27, 42
Louis XII (King), 51
Louvre (Paris), 14, 59
Ludovico, Francesco (Duke), 20, 27–29, 30

M
Machiavelli, Niccolò, 48, 49
machinery, history of, 23
machines of war, 34
machines, inventor of, 11, 18, 25–27
macrocosm, 20, 29, 51, 57
magnet, 37
manuscript, 7, 8
map, 47, 48
Marsyas (Greek God), 14

Martelli, Piero di Braccio, 51
Martesana canal, 27
mathematics, 30, 40–41
Maximillan I (Emperor), 30
Medici family, 7, 8, 13, 49 (QR code)
Mediterranean Sea, 8
Melzi, Francesco (*Il Fanfoia*), 58, 60, 80, 82
Michelangelo, 16, 52, 53
microcosm, 44, 51
Milan, 7, 14, 20–21, 23, 28, 30
Milan Cathedral, 26
military science, theory of, 47
Mirundola, Pico della, 16
models, 42
Mona Lisa, 55, 59, 64 (QR code)
monastery, 45
monk, 22
Mount Albano (Italy), 8
movement, circular, 37
movement, natural, 32, 37
multiple-barreled guns, 25
muscles, 14, 58, 67

N

natural perspective, 34
natural philosophy, 6, 10
Nature, 33, 34, 56–57
nature, role in art, 12
Newton, Issac, 35, 39
notebooks
  illustrations, 17, 24, 27, 39, 40, 50, 55
  research, 18, 21, 23, 28, 36, 47–48, 51, 79

O

optic nerve, 20, 28
optical illusion, 22, 34
orbit, 28
Ottoman Turks, 45

P

Pacioli, Luca, 30, 40–41, 45
paddleboats, 27, 51
paint technique, 52
painting, 7, 20, 23 (QR code)
Palazzo Vecchio, 6, 10, 14, 51–53
percussion, 37, 38, 72
perspective
  rules of, 14, 28, 34, 40
  study of, 12, 14, 16, 22, 28
  theory of, 14
phyllotaxis, 62, 70
physical forces (movement), 37
physiology, 6, 16
Plague (1484), 27–28
plants, 14
Plato, 8, 28
Pollaiuolo, Antonio, 13, 14
The Prince (Machiavelli), 49
principles, 33
projectiles, 25
propeller, 25
proportions, study of, 15
pyramid, 37, 45
pyramidal movement, 37, 39

R

religious doctrine (theology), 33
Renaissance, 7, 8 (QR code), 23 (QR code), 63, 65
Republic of Florence, 13
Reubens, Peter Paul, 53
River Arno (Italy), 8, 14, 48
rock formation, 14
Roman Empire, 13

S

Saint Jerome, 14, 15
Saint John, 75
Salvator, Mundi (Savior of the World), 79
science, 10, 21, 25, 33
science of art, 12, 15, 21
Scotto, Giovanni, 70
sculptor, 11, 58
sculpture, 7, 16, 18
Seracini, Maurizio, 53
Servite brotherhood, 45
Sforza, Ludovico (Duke of Milan), 18, 21, 29, 76
Sforza, Maximilian, 60
shade, 22, 34
Sixtus IV (Pope), 63
sound, 35, 37
Specchi, Giovanni delgi, 64
St.Jerome in the Wilderness, 15, 75
steam-powered gun (Architronito), 25
Summa de arithmetica (Pacioli), 40–41

T
Taccola, 27
terrestrial machine (Earth), 33, 37, 47, 50
theology (religious doctrine), 33
tin, 63
tongue, 23
Toscanelli, Paolo, 13
trail-and-error technology, 25
Treatise on Painting (1651), 82
tremor, 35
truth, artistic representation of, 12
Turkish Ottoman Empire, 9
turn-spit, 25

U
Uffizi Gallery, 14, 18
unbiased observation, 16

V
Vasari, Giorgio, 15, 16, 21, 45, 53, 58, 60
Vatican, 14
vegetarian, 16
Venice, 7, 21, 45
ventricle, 69
Venus, 63
Villa Borghese Gardens (Rome), 68
Vinci (Italy), 8, 10
Virgin and Child with St. Anne and St. John the Baptist, 45, 46–47
Virgin of the Rocks, 22
vision, 25, 34
vital spirit, 62, 65
Vitruvian Man, 32
Vitruvius, 27, 40
vulgar, 74, 76

W
war machines, 18
water power, 26
water wheels, 26
water, movement of, 34–35, 39, 42, 48, 78
water, study of, 26, 34–35
wool trade, 8
writing style, 24

About the Author

John Cashin has written several books for young adults. He served as a military policeman in the U.S. Army, and recently retired after twenty years as a police officer in South Carolina. He lives near McCormick, South Carolina, with his wife Elizabeth.

Photo Credits

Everett Collection: 76; Library of Congress: 17, 24, 27, 51, 71; used under license from Shutterstock, Inc.: 1, 6, 10, 12, 20, 44, 50, 65, 68, 77; Lestertair / shutterstock.com: 9; Lefteris Papaulakis / shutterstock.com: 11; Pen_85 / shutterstock.com: 62; Posztos / shutterstock.com: 29; Massimo Santi / shutterstock.com: 74; Alfonso de Tomas / shutterstock.com: 59; Yuri Turkov / shutterstock.com: 34; Leonard Zhukovsky / shutterstock.com: 79; Luc Viatour / https://Lucnix.be: 32; Wellcome Library: 35, 36, 41, 56, 66, 67, 78; Wikimedia Commons: 15, 22, 46, 47, 53, 81, 85.